THE PENELOPIAD

Also by Margaret Atwood

Fiction

Oryx and Crake (2003)
The Blind Assassin (2000)
Alias Grace (1996)
The Robber Bride (1993)
Good Bones (1992)
Wilderness Tips (1991)
Cat's Eye (1988)
The Handmaid's Tale (1985)
Bluebeard's Egg (1983)
Murder in the Dark (1983)
Bodily Harm (1981)
Life Before Man (1979)
Dancing Girls (1977)
Lady Oracle (1976)
Surfacing (1972)
The Edible Woman (1969)

For Children

Bashful Bob and Doleful Dorinda (2004)
Rude Ramsay and the Roaring Radishes (2003)
Princess Prunella and the Purple Peanut (1995)
For the Birds (1990)
Anna's Pet [with Joyce Barkhouse] (1980)
Up in the Tree (1978)

Non-Fiction

Moving Targets: Writing with Intent 1984–2002 (2004)
Negotiating with the Dead: A Writer on Writing (2002)
Two Solicitudes: Conversations
[with Victor-Lévy Beaulieu] (1998)
Strange Things: The Malevolent North in Canadian Literature (1996)
Second Words (1982)
Days of the Rebels 1815–1840 (1977)
Survival: A Thematic Guide to Canadian Literature (1972)

Poetry

Morning in the Burned House (1995)
Selected Poems II: Poems Selected and New 1976–1986 (1986)
Interlunar (1984)
True Stories (1981)
Two-Headed Poems (1978)
Selected Poems (1976)
You Are Happy (1974)
Power Politics (1971)
Procedures for Underground (1970)
The Journals of Susanna Moodie (1970)
The Animals in That Country (1968)
The Circle Game (1966)
Double Persephone (1961)

Myths are universal and timeless stories that reflect and shape our lives – they explore our desires, our fears, our longings, and provide narratives that remind us what it means to be human. *The Myths* series brings together some of the world's finest writers, each of whom has retold a myth in a contemporary and memorable way. Authors in the series include: Chinua Achebe, Margaret Atwood, Karen Armstrong, AS Byatt, David Grossman, Milton Hatoum, Victor Pelevin, Donna Tartt, Su Tong and Jeanette Winterson..

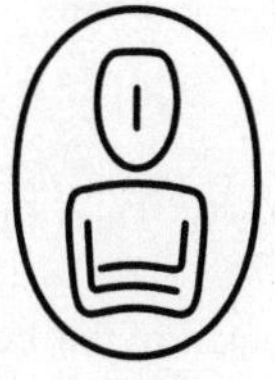

THE PENELOPIAD

Margaret Atwood

CANONGATE
Edinburgh · New York · Melbourne

First published in Great Britain in 2005 by
Canongate Books Ltd., Edinburgh, Scotland

Printed in the United States of America

ISBN-13: 978-1-84195-798-2

Canongate
841 Broadway
New York, NY 10003

Distributed by Publishers Group West

www.groveatlantic.com

12 13 14 15 10 9 8

For my family

'. . . Shrewd Odysseus! . . . You are a fortunate man to have won a wife of such pre-eminent virtue! How faithful was your flawless Penelope, Icarius' daughter! How loyally she kept the memory of the husband of her youth! The glory of her virtue will not fade with the years, but the deathless gods themselves will make a beautiful song for mortal ears in honour of the constant Penelope.'

– *The Odyssey*, Book 24 (191–194)

. . . he took a cable which had seen service on a blue-bowed ship, made one end fast to a high column in the portico, and threw the other over the round-house, high up, so that their feet would not touch the ground. As when long-winged thrushes or doves get entangled in a snare . . . so the women's heads were held fast in a row, with nooses round their necks, to bring them to the most pitiable end. For a little while their feet twitched, but not for very long.

– *The Odyssey*, Book 22 (470–473)

CONTENTS

Introduction

The story of Odysseus' return to his home kingdom of Ithaca following an absence of twenty years is best known from Homer's *Odyssey*. Odysseus is said to have spent half of these years fighting the Trojan War and the other half wandering around the Aegean Sea, trying to get home, enduring hardships, conquering or evading monsters, and sleeping with goddesses. The character of 'wily Odysseus' has been much commented on: he's noted as a persuasive liar and disguise artist – a man who lives by his wits, who devises stratagems and tricks, and who is sometimes too clever for his own good. His divine helper is Pallas Athene, a goddess who admires Odysseus for his ready inventiveness.

In *The Odyssey*, Penelope – daughter of Icarius of Sparta, and cousin of the beautiful Helen of Troy – is portrayed as the quintessential faithful wife, a woman known for her intelligence and constancy. In addition to weeping and praying for the return of Odysseus, she cleverly deceives the many Suitors who are swarming around her palace, eating up Odysseus' estate in an attempt to force her to marry one of them. Not only does Penelope lead them on with false promises, she weaves a shroud that she unravels at night, delaying her marriage decision until its completion. Part of *The Odyssey* concerns her problems with her teenaged son, Telemachus, who is bent on asserting himself not only against the troublesome and dangerous Suitors, but against his mother as well. The book draws to an end with the slaughter of the Suitors by Odysseus and Telemachus, the hanging of twelve of the maids who have been sleeping with the Suitors, and the reunion of Odysseus and Penelope.

But Homer's *Odyssey* is not the only version of the story. Mythic material was originally oral, and also local – a myth would be told one way in one place and quite differently in another. I have drawn on material other than *The Odyssey*, especially for the details of Penelope's parentage, her early life and marriage, and the scandalous rumours circulating about her.

I've chosen to give the telling of the story to Penelope and to the twelve hanged maids. The maids form a chanting and singing Chorus which focuses on two questions that must pose themselves after any close reading of *The Odyssey*: what led to the hanging of the maids, and what was Penelope really up to? The story as told in *The Odyssey* doesn't hold water: there are too many inconsistencies. I've always been haunted by the hanged maids; and, in *The Penelopiad*, so is Penelope herself.

i

A Low Art

Now that I'm dead I know everything. This is what I wished would happen, but like so many of my wishes it failed to come true. I know only a few factoids that I didn't know before. Death is much too high a price to pay for the satisfaction of curiosity, needless to say.

Since being dead – since achieving this state of bonelessness, liplessness, breastlessness – I've learned some things I would rather not know, as one does when listening at windows or opening other people's letters. You think you'd like to read minds? Think again.

Down here everyone arrives with a sack, like the sacks used to keep the winds in, but each of these sacks is full of words – words you've spoken, words you've heard, words that have been said about you. Some sacks are very small, others large; my own is of a reasonable size, though a lot of the words in it concern my eminent husband. What a fool he made of me, some say. It was a specialty of his: making fools. He got away with everything, which was another of his specialties: getting away.

He was always so plausible. Many people have believed that his version of events was the true one, give or take a few murders, a few beautiful seductresses, a few one-eyed monsters. Even I believed him, from time to time. I knew he was tricky and a liar, I just didn't think he would play his tricks and try out his lies on me. Hadn't I been faithful? Hadn't I waited, and waited, and waited, despite the temptation – almost the compulsion – to do otherwise? And what did I amount to, once the official version gained ground? An edifying legend. A stick used to beat other women with. Why couldn't they be as considerate, as trustworthy, as all-suffering as I had been? That was the line they took, the singers, the yarn-spinners. *Don't follow my example*, I want to scream in your ears – yes, yours! But when I try to scream, I sound like an owl.

Of course I had inklings, about his slipperiness, his wiliness, his foxiness, his – how can I put this? – his unscrupulousness, but I turned a blind eye. I kept my mouth shut; or, if I opened it, I sang his praises. I didn't contradict, I didn't ask awkward questions, I didn't dig deep. I wanted happy endings in those days, and happy endings are best achieved by keeping the right doors locked and going to sleep during the rampages.

But after the main events were over and things had become less legendary, I realised how many people were laughing at me behind my back – how they were jeering, making jokes about me, jokes both clean and dirty; how they were turning me into a story, or into several stories, though not the kind of stories I'd prefer to hear about myself. What can a woman do when scandalous gossip travels the world? If she defends herself she sounds guilty. So I waited some more.

Now that all the others have run out of air, it's my turn to do a little story-making. I owe it to myself. I've had to work myself up to it: it's a low art, tale-telling. Old women go in for it, strolling beggars, blind singers, maidservants, children – folks with time on their hands. Once, people would have laughed if I'd tried to play the minstrel – there's nothing more preposterous than an aristocrat fumbling around with the arts – but who cares about public opinion now? The opinion of the people down here: the opinion of shadows, of echoes. So I'll spin a thread of my own.

The difficulty is that I have no mouth through which I can speak. I can't make myself understood, not in your world, the world of bodies, of tongues and fingers; and most of the time I have no listeners, not on your side of the river. Those of you who may catch the odd whisper, the odd squeak, so easily mistake my words for breezes rustling the dry reeds, for bats at twilight, for bad dreams.

But I've always been of a determined nature. Patient, they used to call me. I like to see a thing through to the end.

ii

The Chorus Line:
A Rope-Jumping Rhyme

we are the maids
the ones you killed
the ones you failed

we danced in air
our bare feet twitched
it was not fair

with every goddess, queen, and bitch
from there to here
you scratched your itch

we did much less
than what you did
you judged us bad

you had the spear
you had the word
at your command

we scrubbed the blood
of our dead
paramours from floors, from chairs

from stairs, from doors,
we knelt in water
while you stared

at our bare feet
it was not fair
you licked our fear

it gave you pleasure
you raised your hand
you watched us fall

we danced on air
the ones you failed
the ones you killed

iii

My Childhood

Where shall I begin? There are only two choices: at the beginning or not at the beginning. The real beginning would be the beginning of the world, after which one thing has led to another; but since there are differences of opinion about that, I'll begin with my own birth.

My father was King Icarius of Sparta. My mother was a Naiad. Daughters of Naiads were a dime a dozen in those days; the place was crawling with them. Nevertheless, it never hurts to be of semi-divine birth. Or it never hurts immediately.

When I was quite young my father ordered me to be thrown into the sea. I never knew exactly why, during my lifetime, but now I suspect he'd been told by an oracle that I would weave his shroud. Possibly he thought that if he killed me first, his shroud would never be woven and he would live forever. I can see how the reasoning might have gone. In that case, his wish to drown me came from an understandable desire to protect himself. But he must have misheard, or else the oracle herself misheard – the gods often mumble – because it was not his shroud that was at issue, but my father-in-law's shroud. If that was the prophecy it was a true one, and indeed the weaving of this particular shroud proved a great convenience to me later on in my life.

The teaching of crafts to girls has fallen out of fashion now, I understand, but luckily it had not in my day. It's always an advantage to have something to do with your hands. That way, if someone makes an inappropriate remark, you can pretend you haven't heard it. Then you don't have to answer.

But perhaps this shroud-weaving oracle idea of mine is baseless. Perhaps I have only invented it in order to make myself feel better. So much whispering goes on, in the dark caverns, in the meadows, that sometimes it's hard to know whether the whispering is coming from others or from the inside of your own head. I use *head* figuratively. We have dispensed with heads as such, down here.

No matter – into the sea I was thrown. Do I remember the waves closing over me, do I remember the breath leaving my lungs and the sound of bells people say the drowning hear? Not in the least. But I was told the story: there is always some servant or slave or old nurse or busybody ready to regale a child with the awful things done to it by its parents when it was too young to remember. Hearing this discouraging anecdote did not improve my relations with my father. It is to this episode – or rather, to my knowledge of it – that I attribute my reserve, as well as my mistrust of other people's intentions.

It was stupid of Icarius to try to drown the daughter of a Naiad, however. Water is our element, it is our birthright. Although we are not such good swimmers as our mothers, we do have a way of floating, and we're well connected among the fish and seabirds. A flock of purple-striped ducks came to my rescue and towed me ashore. After an omen like that, what could my father do? He took me back, and renamed me – *duck* was my new nickname. No doubt he felt guilty about what he'd almost done: he became, if anything, rather too affectionate towards me.

I found this affection difficult to reciprocate. You can imagine. There I would be, strolling hand in hand with my apparently fond male parent along a cliff edge or a river bank or a parapet, and the thought would occur to me that he might suddenly decide to shove me over or bash me to death with a rock. Preserving a calm façade under these circumstances was a challenge. After such excursions I would retire to my room and dissolve in floods of tears. (Excessive weeping, I might as well tell you now, is a handicap of the Naiad-born. I spent at least a quarter of my earthly life crying my eyes out. Fortunately in my time there were veils. They were a practical help for disguising red, puffy eyes.)

My mother, like all Naiads, was beautiful, but chilly at heart. She had waving hair and dimples, and rippling laughter. She was elusive. When I was little I often tried to throw my arms around her, but she had a habit of sliding away. I like to think that she may have been responsible for calling up that flock of ducks, but probably she wasn't: she preferred swimming in the river to the care of small children, and I often slipped her mind. If my father hadn't had me thrown into the sea she might have dropped me in herself, in a fit of absent-mindedness or irritation. She had a short attention span and rapidly changing emotions.

You can see by what I've told you that I was a child who learned early the virtues – if such they are – of self-sufficiency. I knew that I would have to look out for myself in the world. I could hardly count on family support.

iv

The Chorus Line: Kiddie Mourn, A Lament by the Maids

We too were children. We too were born to the wrong parents. Poor parents, slave parents, peasant parents, and serf parents; parents who sold us, parents from whom we were stolen. These parents were not gods, they were not demi-gods, they were not nymphs or Naiads. We were set to work in the palace, as children; we drudged from dawn to dusk, as children. If we wept, no one dried our tears. If we slept, we were kicked awake. We were told we were motherless. We were told we were fatherless. We were told we were lazy. We were told we were dirty. We were dirty. Dirt was our concern, dirt was our business, dirt was our specialty, dirt was our fault. We were the dirty girls. If our owners or the sons of our owners or a visiting nobleman or the sons of a visiting nobleman wanted to sleep with us, we could not refuse. It did us no good to weep, it did us no good to say we were in pain. All this happened to us when we were children. If we were pretty children our lives were worse. We ground the flour for lavish wedding feasts, then we ate the leftovers; we would never have a wedding feast of our own, no rich gifts would be exchanged for us; our bodies had little value. But we wanted to sing and dance too, we wanted to be happy too. As we grew older we became polished and evasive, we mastered the secret sneer. We swayed our hips, we lurked, we winked, we signalled with our eyebrows, even when we were children; we met boys behind the pigpens, noble boys and ignoble boys alike. We rolled around in the straw, in the mud, in the dung, on the beds of soft fleece we were making up for our masters. We drank the wine left in the wine cups. We spat onto the serving platters. Between the bright hall and the dark scullery we crammed filched meat into our mouths. We laughed together in our attics, in our nights. We snatched what we could.

V

Asphodel

It's dark here, as many have remarked. 'Dark Death', they used to say. 'The gloomy halls of Hades', and so forth. Well, yes, it is dark, but there are advantages – for instance, if you see someone you'd rather not speak to you can always pretend you haven't recognised them.

There are of course the fields of asphodel. You can walk around in them if you want. It's brighter there, and a certain amount of vapid dancing goes on, though the region sounds better than it is – *the fields of asphodel* has a poetic lilt to it. But just consider. Asphodel, asphodel, asphodel – pretty enough white flowers, but a person gets tired of them after a while. It would have been better to supply some variety – an assortment of colours, a few winding paths and vistas and stone benches and fountains. I would have preferred the odd hyacinth, at least, and would a sprinkling of crocuses have been too much to expect? Though we never get spring here, or any other seasons. You do have to wonder who designed the place.

Have I mentioned the fact that there's nothing to eat except asphodel?

But I shouldn't complain.

The darker grottoes are more interesting – the conversation there is better, if you can find a minor rascal of some sort – a pickpocket, a stockbroker, a small-time pimp. Like a lot of goody-goody girls, I was always secretly attracted to men of that kind.

I don't frequent the really deep levels much, though. That's where the punishments are dealt out to the truly villainous, those who were not sufficiently punished while alive. It's hard to put up with the screams. The torture is mental torture, however, since we don't have bodies any more. What the gods really like is to conjure up banquets – big platters of meat, heaps of bread, bunches of grapes – and then snatch them away. Making people roll heavy stones up steep hills is another of their favourite jests. I sometimes have a yen to go down there: it might help me to remember what it was like to have real hunger, what it was like to have real fatigue.

Every once in a while the fogs part and we get a glimpse of the world of the living. It's like rubbing the glass on a dirty window, making a space to look through. Sometimes the barrier dissolves and we can go on an outing. Then we get very excited, and there is a great deal of squeaking.

These outings can take place in many ways. Once upon a time, anyone who wished to consult us would slit the throat of a sheep or cow or pig and let the blood flow into a trench in the ground. We'd smell it and make a beeline for the site, like flies to a carcass. There we'd be, chirping and fluttering, thousands of us, like the contents of a giant wastepaper basket caught in a tornado, while some self-styled hero held us off with drawn sword until the one he wanted to consult appeared. A few vague prophecies would be forthcoming: we learned to keep them vague. Why tell everything? You needed to keep them coming back for more, with other sheep, cows, pigs, and so forth.

Once the right number of words had been handed over to the hero we'd all be allowed to drink from the trench, and I can't say much in praise of the table manners on such occasions. There was a lot of pushing and shoving, a lot of slurping and spilling; there were a lot of crimson chins. However, it was glorious to feel the blood coursing in our non-existent veins again, if only for an instant.

We could sometimes appear as dreams, though that wasn't as satisfactory. Then there were those who got stuck on the wrong side of the river because they hadn't been given proper burials. They wandered around in a very unhappy state, neither here nor there, and they could cause a lot of trouble.

Then after hundreds, possibly thousands of years – it's hard to keep track of time here, because we don't have any of it as such – customs changed. No living people went to the underworld much any more, and our own abode was upstaged by a much more spectacular establishment down the road –

fiery pits, wailing and gnashing of teeth, gnawing worms, demons with pitchforks – a great many special effects.

But we were still called up occasionally by magicians and conjurors – men who'd made pacts with the infernal powers – and then by smaller fry, the table-tilters, the mediums, the channellers, people of that ilk. It was demeaning, all of it – to have to materialise in a chalk circle or a velvet-upholstered parlour just because someone wanted to gape at you – but it did allow us to keep up with what was going on among the still-alive. I was very interested in the invention of the light bulb, for instance, and in the matter-into-energy theories of the twentieth century. More recently, some of us have been able to infiltrate the new ethereal-wave system that now encircles the globe, and to travel around that way, looking out at the world through the flat, illuminated surfaces that serve as domestic shrines. Perhaps that's how the gods were able to come and go as quickly as they did back then – they must have had something like that at their disposal.

I never got summoned much by the magicians. I was famous, yes – ask anyone – but for some reason they didn't want to see me, whereas my cousin Helen was much in demand. It didn't seem fair – I wasn't known for doing anything notorious, especially of a sexual nature, and she was nothing if not infamous. Of course she was very beautiful. It was claimed she'd come out of an egg, being the daughter of Zeus who'd raped her mother in the form of a swan. She was quite stuck-up about it, was Helen. I wonder how many of us really believed that swan-rape concoction? There were a lot of stories of that kind going around then – the gods couldn't seem to keep their hands or paws or beaks off mortal women, they were always raping someone or other.

Anyway, the magicians insisted on seeing Helen, and she was willing to oblige. It was like a return to the old days to have a lot of men gawping at her. She liked to appear in one of her Trojan outfits, over-decorated to my taste, but *chacun à son goût*. She had a kind of slow twirl she would do; then she'd lower her head and glance up into the face of whoever had conjured her up, and give one of her trademark intimate smiles, and they were hers. Or she'd take on the form in which she displayed herself to her outraged husband, Menelaus, when Troy was burning and he was about to plunge his vengeful sword into her. All she had to do was bare one of her peerless breasts, and he was down on his knees, and drooling and begging to take her back.

As for me . . . well, people told me I was beautiful, they had to tell me that because I was a princess, and shortly after that a queen, but the truth was that although I was not deformed or ugly, I was nothing special to look at. I was smart, though: considering the times, very smart. That seems to be what I was known for: being smart. That, and my weaving, and my devotion to my husband, and my discretion.

If you were a magician, messing around in the dark arts and risking your soul, would you want to conjure up a plain but smart wife who'd been good at weaving and had never transgressed, instead of a woman who'd driven hundreds of men mad with lust and had caused a great city to go up in flames?

Neither would I.

Helen was never punished, not one bit. Why not, I'd like to know? Other people got strangled by sea serpents and drowned in storms and turned into spiders and shot with arrows for much smaller crimes. Eating the wrong cows. Boasting. That sort of thing. You'd think Helen might have got a good whipping at the very least, after all the harm and suffering she caused to countless other people. But she didn't.

Not that I mind.

Not that I minded.

I had other things in my life to occupy my attention.

Which brings me to the subject of my marriage.

vi

My Marriage

My marriage was arranged. That's the way things were done then: where there were weddings, there were arrangements. I don't mean such things as bridal outfits, flowers, banquets, and music, though we had those too. Everyone has those, even now. The arrangements I mean were more devious than that.

Under the old rules only important people had marriages, because only important people had inheritances. All the rest was just copulation of various kinds – rapes or seductions, love affairs or one-night stands, with gods who said they were shepherds or shepherds who said they were gods. Occasionally a goddess might get mixed up in it too, dabble around in perishable flesh like a queen playing at milkmaids, but the reward for the man was a shortened life and often a violent death.

Immortality and mortality didn't mix well: it was fire and mud, only the fire always won.

The gods were never averse to making a mess. In fact they enjoyed it. To watch some mortal with his or her eyes frying in their sockets through an overdose of god-sex made them shake with laughter. There was something childish about the gods, in a nasty way. I can say this now because I no longer have a body, I'm beyond that kind of suffering, and the gods aren't listening anyway. As far as I can tell they've gone to sleep. In your world, you don't get visitations from the gods the way people used to unless you're on drugs.

Where was I? Oh yes. Marriages. Marriages were for having children, and children were not toys and pets. Children were vehicles for passing things along. These things could be kingdoms, rich wedding gifts, stories, grudges, blood feuds. Through children, alliances were forged; through children, wrongs were avenged. To have a child was to set loose a force in the world.

If you had an enemy it was best to kill his sons,

even if those sons were babies. Otherwise they would grow up and hunt you down. If you couldn't bring yourself to slaughter them, you could disguise them and send them far away, or sell them as slaves, but as long as they were alive they would be a danger to you.

If you had daughters instead of sons, you needed to get them bred as soon as possible so you could have grandsons. The more sword-wielders and spear-throwers you could count on from within your family the better, because all the other noteworthy men around were on the lookout for a pretext to raid some king or noble and carry away anything they could grab, people included. Weakness in one power-holder meant opportunity for another, so every king and noble needed all the help he could get.

Thus it went without saying that a marriage would be arranged for me when the time came.

At the court of King Icarius, my father, they still retained the ancient custom of having contests to see who should marry a nobly born woman who was – so to speak – on the block. The man who won the contest got the woman and the wedding, and was then expected to stay at the bride's father's palace and contribute his share of male offspring. He obtained wealth through the marriage – gold cups, silver bowls, horses, robes, weapons, all that trash they used to value so much back when I was alive. His family was expected to hand over a lot of this trash as well.

I can say *trash* because I know where most of it ended up. It mouldered away in the ground or it sank to the bottom of the sea, or it got broken or melted down. Some of it made its way to enormous palaces that have – strangely – no kings or queens in them. Endless processions of people in graceless clothing file through these palaces, staring at the gold cups and the silver bowls, which are not even used any more. Then they go to a sort of market inside the palace and buy pictures of these things, or miniature versions of them that are not real silver and gold. That is why I say *trash*.

Under the ancient customs, the huge pile of sparkling wedding loot stayed with the bride's family, in the bride's family's palace. Perhaps that is why my father had become so attached to me after having failed to drown me in the sea: where I was, there would be the treasure.

(Why *did* he throw me in? That question still haunts me. Although I'm not altogether satisfied with the shroud-weaving explanation, I've never been able to find the right answer, even down here. Every time I see my father in the distance, wading through the asphodel, and try to catch up with him, he hurries away as if he doesn't want to face me.

I've sometimes thought I may have been a sacrifice to the god of the sea, who was known to be thirsty for human life. Then the ducks rescued me, through no act of my father's. I suppose my father could argue that he'd fulfilled his side of the bargain, if bargain it was, and that he hadn't cheated, and that if the sea-god had failed to drag me down and devour me, that was his own tough luck.

The more I think about this version of events, the more I like it. It makes sense.)

Picture me, then, as a clever but not overly beautiful girl of marriageable age, let's say fifteen. Suppose I'm looking out the window of my room – which was on the second floor of the palace – down into the courtyard where the contestants are gathering: all those young hopefuls who wish to compete for my hand.

I don't look directly out of the window, of course. I don't plant my elbows on the windowsill like some hulking maid and stare shamelessly. No, I peek, from behind my veil and from behind the drapery. It would not do to let all those scantily clad young men see my unveiled face. The palace women have dolled me up as best they can, minstrels have composed songs of praise in my honour – 'radiant as Aphrodite', and all the usual claptrap – but I feel shy and miserable. The young men laugh and joke; they seem at ease with one another; they do not glance up.

I know it isn't me they're after, not Penelope the

Duck. It's only what comes with me – the royal connection, the pile of glittering junk. No man will ever kill himself for love of me.

And no man ever did. Not that I would have wanted to inspire those kinds of suicides. I was not a man-eater, I was not a Siren, I was not like cousin Helen who loved to make conquests just to show she could. As soon as the man was grovelling, and it never took long, she'd stroll away without a backwards glance, giving that careless laugh of hers, as if she'd just been watching the palace midget standing ridiculously on his head.

I was a kind girl – kinder than Helen, or so I thought. I knew I would have to have something to offer instead of beauty. I was clever, everyone said so – in fact they said it so much that I found it discouraging – but cleverness is a quality a man likes to have in his wife as long as she is some distance away from him. Up close, he'll take kindness any day of the week, if there's nothing more alluring to be had.

The most obvious husband for me would have been a younger son of a king with large estates – one of King Nestor's boys, perhaps. That would have been a good connection for King Icarius. Through my veil, I studied the young men milling around down below, trying to figure out who each one was and – a thing of no practical consequence, since it wasn't up to me to choose my husband – which one I preferred.

A couple of the maids were with me – they never left me unattended, I was a risk until I was safely married, because who knew what upstart fortune hunter might try to seduce me or seize me and run away with me? The maids were my sources of information. They were ever-flowing fountains of trivial gossip: they could come and go freely in the palace, they could study the men from all angles, they could listen in on their conversations, they could laugh and joke with them as much as they pleased: no one cared who might worm his way in between their legs.

'Who's the barrel-chested one?' I asked.

'Oh, that's only Odysseus,' said one of the maids. He was not considered – by the maids at least – to be a serious candidate for my hand. His father's palace was on Ithaca, a goat-strewn rock; his clothes were rustic; he had the manners of a small-town big shot, and had already expressed several complicated ideas the others considered peculiar. He was clever though, they said. In fact he was too clever for his own good. The other young men made jokes about him – 'Don't gamble with Odysseus, the friend of Hermes,' they said. 'You'll never win.' This was like saying he was a cheat and a thief. His grandfather Autolycus was well known for these very qualities, and was reputed never to have won anything fairly in his life.

'I wonder how fast he can run,' I said. In some kingdoms the contest for brides was a wrestling match, in others a chariot race, but with us it was just running.

'Not very fast, on those short legs of his,' said one maid unkindly. And indeed the legs of Odysseus were quite short in relation to his body. It was all right when he was sitting down, you didn't notice, but standing up he looked top-heavy.

'Not fast enough to catch *you*,' said another of the maids. 'You wouldn't want to wake up in the morning and find yourself in bed with your husband and a herd of Apollo's cows.' This was a joke about Hermes, whose first act of thievery on the day he was born involved an audacious cattle raid. 'Not unless one of them was a bull,' said another. 'Or else a goat,' said a third. 'A big strong ram! I bet our young duck would like that! She'd be bleating soon enough!' 'I wouldn't mind one of that kind myself,' said a fourth. 'Better a ram than the babyfingers you get around here.' They all began laughing, holding their hands over their mouths and snorting with mirth.

I was mortified. I didn't understand the coarser kinds of jokes, not yet, so I didn't know exactly why they were laughing, though I understood that their laughter was at my expense. But I had no way of making them stop.

* * *

At this moment my cousin Helen came sailing up, like the long-necked swan she fancied herself to be. She had a distinctive swaying walk and she was exaggerating it. Although mine was the marriage in question, she wanted all the attention for herself. She was as beautiful as usual, indeed more so: she was intolerably beautiful. She was dressed to perfection: Menelaus, her husband, always made sure of that, and he was rich as stink so he could afford it. She tilted her face towards me, looking at me whimsically as if she were flirting. I suspect she used to flirt with her dog, with her mirror, with her comb, with her bedpost. She needed to keep in practice.

'I think Odysseus would make a very suitable husband for our little duckie,' she said. 'She likes the quiet life, and she'll certainly have that if he takes her to Ithaca, as he's boasting of doing. She can help him look after his goats. She and Odysseus are two of a kind. They both have such short legs.' She said this lightly, but her lightest sayings were often her cruellest. Why is it that really beautiful people think everyone else in the world exists merely for their amusement?

The maids sniggered. I was crushed. I had not thought my legs were quite that short, and I certainly hadn't thought Helen would notice them. But not much escaped her when it came to assessing the physical graces and defects of others. That was what got her into trouble with Paris, later – he was so much better looking than Menelaus, who was lumpish and red-haired. The best that was claimed of Menelaus, once they started putting him into the poems, was that he had a very loud voice.

The maids all looked at me to see what I would say. But Helen had a way of leaving people speechless, and I was no exception.

'Never mind, little cousin,' she said to me, patting me on the arm. 'They say he's very clever. And you're very clever too, they tell me. So you'll be able to understand what he says. I certainly never could! It was lucky for both of us that he didn't win *me*!'

She gave the patronizing smirk of someone who's

had first chance at a less than delicious piece of sausage but has fastidiously rejected it. Indeed, Odysseus had been among the suitors for her hand, and like every other man on earth he'd desperately wanted to win her. Now he was competing for what was at best only second prize.

Helen strolled away, having delivered her sting. The maids began discussing her splendid necklace, her scintillating earrings, her perfect nose, her elegant hairstyle, her luminous eyes, the tastefully woven border of her shining robe. It was as if I wasn't there. And it was my wedding day.

All of this was a strain on the nerves. I started to cry, as I would do so often in the future, and was taken to lie down on my bed.

Thus I missed the race itself. Odysseus won it. He cheated, as I later learned. My father's brother, Uncle Tyndareus, father of Helen – though, as I've told you, some said that Zeus was her real father – helped him to do it. He mixed the wine of the other contestants with a drug that slowed them down, though not so much as they would notice; to Odysseus he gave a potion that had the opposite effect. I understand that this sort of thing has become a tradition, and is still practised in the world of the living when it comes to athletic contests.

Why did Uncle Tyndareus help my future husband in this way? They were neither friends nor allies. What did Tyndareus stand to gain? My uncle would not have helped anyone – believe me – simply out of the goodness of his heart, a commodity that was in short supply.

One story has it that I was the payment for a service Odysseus had rendered to Tyndareus. When they were all competing for Helen and things were getting more and more angry, Odysseus made each contestant swear an oath that whoever won Helen must be defended by all of the others if any other man tried to take her away from the winner. In that way he calmed things down and allowed the match with Menelaus to proceed smoothly. He must have known he had no hope himself. It was then – so the rumour goes – that he struck the bargain with Tyndareus: in return for assuring a peaceful and very profitable wedding for the radiant Helen, Odysseus would get plain-Jane Penelope.

But I have another idea, and here it is. Tyndareus and my father, Icarius, were both kings of Sparta. They were supposed to rule alternately, one for a year and the other the next, turn and turn about. But Tyndareus wanted the throne for himself alone, and indeed he later got it. It would stand to reason that he'd sounded out the various suitors on their prospects and their plans, and had learned that Odysseus shared the newfangled idea that the wife should go to the husband's family rather than the other way around. It would suit Tyndareus fine if I could be sent far away, me and any sons I might bear. That way there would be fewer to come to the aid of Icarius in the event of an open conflict.

Whatever was behind it, Odysseus cheated and won the race. I saw Helen smiling maliciously as she watched the marriage rites. She thought I was being pawned off on an uncouth dolt who would haul me off to a dreary backwater, and she was not displeased. She'd probably known well beforehand that the fix was in.

As for me, I had trouble making it through the ceremony – the sacrifices of animals, the offerings to the gods, the lustral sprinklings, the libations, the prayers, the interminable songs. I felt quite dizzy. I kept my eyes downcast, so all I could see of Odysseus was the lower part of his body. *Short legs*, I kept thinking, even at the most solemn moments. This was not an appropriate thought – it was trivial and silly, and it made me want to giggle – but in my own defence I must point out that I was only fifteen.

vii

The Scar

And so I was handed over to Odysseus, like a package of meat. A package of meat in a wrapping of gold, mind you. A sort of gilded blood pudding.

But perhaps that is too crude a simile for you. Let me add that meat was highly valued among us – the aristocracy ate lots of it, meat, meat, meat, and all they ever did was roast it: ours was not an age of haute cuisine. Oh, I forgot: there was also bread, flatbread that is, bread, bread, bread, and wine, wine, wine. We did have the odd fruit or vegetable, but you've probably never heard of these because no one put them into the songs much.

The gods wanted meat as much as we did, but all they ever got from us was the bones and fat, thanks to a bit of rudimentary sleight of hand by Prometheus: only an idiot would have been deceived by a bag of bad cow parts disguised as good ones, and Zeus was deceived; which goes to show that the gods were not always as intelligent as they wanted us to believe.

I can say this now because I'm dead. I wouldn't have dared to say it earlier. You could never tell when one of the gods might be listening, disguised as a beggar or an old friend or a stranger. It's true that I sometimes doubted their existence, these gods. But during my lifetime I considered it prudent not to take any risks.

There was lots of everything at my wedding feast – great glistening hunks of meat, great wads of fragrant bread, great flagons of mellow wine. It was amazing that the guests didn't burst on the spot, they stuffed themselves so full. Nothing helps gluttony along so well as eating food you don't have to pay for yourself, as I learned from later experience.

We ate with our hands in those days. There was a lot of gnawing and some heavy-duty chewing, but it was better that way – no sharp utensils that could be snatched up and plunged into a fellow guest who might have annoyed you. At any wedding preceded by a contest there were bound to be a few sore losers; but no unsuccessful suitor lost his temper at my feast. It was more as if they'd failed to win an auction for a horse.

The wine was mixed too strong, so there were many fuddled heads. Even my father, King Icarius, got quite drunk. He suspected he'd had a trick played on him by Tyndareus and Odysseus, he was almost sure they'd cheated, but he couldn't figure out how they'd done it; and this made him angry, and when he was angry he drank even more, and dropped insulting comments about people's grandparents. But he was a king, so there were no duels.

Odysseus himself did not get drunk. He had a way of appearing to drink a lot without actually doing it. He told me later that if a man lives by his wits, as he did, he needs to have those wits always at hand and kept sharp, like axes or swords. Only fools, he said, were given to bragging about how much they could drink. It was bound to lead to swilling competitions, and then to inattention and the loss of one's powers, and that would be when your enemy would strike.

As for me, I couldn't eat a thing. I was too nervous. I sat there shrouded in my bridal veil, hardly daring to glance at Odysseus. I was certain he would be disappointed in me once he'd lifted that veil and made his way in through the cloak and the girdle and the shimmering robe in which I'd been decked out. But he wasn't looking at me, and neither was anyone else. They were all staring at Helen, who was dispensing dazzling smiles right and left, not missing a single man. She had a way of smiling that made each one of them feel that secretly she was in love with him alone.

I suppose it was lucky that Helen was distracting everyone's attention, because it kept them from noticing me and my trembling and awkwardness. I wasn't just nervous, I was really afraid. The maids had been filling my ears with tales about how – once I was in the bridal chamber – I would be torn apart as the earth is by the plough, and how painful and humiliating that would be.

As for my mother, she'd stopped swimming around like a porpoise long enough to attend my wedding, for which I was less grateful than I ought to have been. There she sat on her throne beside my father, robed in cool blue, a small puddle gathering at her feet. She did make a little speech to me as the maids were changing my costume yet again, but I didn't consider it to be a helpful one at the time. It was nothing if not oblique; but then, all Naiads are oblique.

Here is what she said:

Water does not resist. Water flows. When you plunge your hand into it, all you feel is a caress. Water is not a solid wall, it will not stop you. But water always goes where it wants to go, and nothing in the end can stand against it. Water is patient. Dripping water wears away a stone. Remember that, my child. Remember you are half water. If you can't go through an obstacle, go around it. Water does.

After the ceremonies and the feasting, there was the usual procession to the bridal chamber, with the usual torches and vulgar jokes and drunken yelling. The bed had been garlanded, the threshold sprinkled, the libations poured. The gatekeeper had been posted to keep the bride from rushing out in horror, and to stop her friends from breaking down the door and rescuing her when they heard her scream. All of this was play-acting: the fiction was that the bride had been stolen, and the consummation of a marriage was supposed to be a sanctioned rape. It was supposed to be a conquest, a trampling of a foe, a mock killing. There was supposed to be blood.

Once the door had been closed, Odysseus took me by the hand and sat me down on the bed. 'Forget everything you've been told,' he whispered. 'I'm not going to hurt you, or not very much. But it would help us both if you could pretend. I've been told you're a clever girl. Do you think you could manage a few screams? That will satisfy them – they're listening at the door – and then they'll leave us in peace and we can take our time to become friends.'

This was one of his great secrets as a persuader – he could convince another person that the two of them together faced a common obstacle, and that they needed to join forces in order to overcome it. He could draw almost any listener into a collaboration, a little conspiracy of his own making. Nobody could do this better than he: for once, the stories don't lie. And he had a wonderful voice as well, deep and sonorous. So of course I did as he asked.

Somewhat later I found that Odysseus was not one of those men who, after the act, simply roll over and begin to snore. Not that I am aware of this common male habit through my own experience; but as I've said, I listened a lot to the maids. No, Odysseus wanted to talk, and as he was an excellent raconteur I was happy to listen. I think this is what he valued most in me: my ability to appreciate his stories. It's an underrated talent in women.

I'd had occasion to notice the long scar on his thigh, and so he proceeded to tell me the story of how he got it. As I've already mentioned, his grandfather was Autolycus, who claimed the god Hermes was his father. That may have been a way of saying that he was a crafty old thief, cheat, and liar, and that luck had favoured him in these kinds of activities.

Autolycus was the father of Odysseus's mother, Anticleia, who'd married King Laertes of Ithaca and was therefore now my mother-in-law. There was a slanderous item going around about Anticleia – that she'd been seduced by Sisyphus, who was the true father of Odysseus – but I found it difficult to believe, as who would want to seduce Anticleia? It would be like seducing a prow. But let the tale stand, for the moment.

Sisyphus was a man so tricky he was said to have cheated Death twice: once by fooling King Hades into putting on handcuffs that Sisyphus refused to unlock, once by talking Persephone into letting him out of the underworld because he hadn't been properly buried, and thus didn't belong on the dead side of the River Styx. So if we admit the rumour about

Anticleia's infidelity, Odysseus had crafty and unscrupulous men on two of the main branches of his family tree.

Whatever the truth of this, his grandfather Autolycus – who'd named him – invited Odysseus to Mount Parnassus to collect the gifts promised him at his birth. Odysseus did pay the visit, during which he went boar hunting with the sons of Autolycus. It was a particularly ferocious boar that had gored him in the thigh and given him the scar.

There was something in the way Odysseus told the story that made me suspect there was more to it. Why had the boar savaged Odysseus, but not the others? Had they known where the boar was hiding out, had they led him into a trap? Was Odysseus meant to die so that Autolycus the cheat wouldn't have to hand over the gifts he owed? Perhaps.

I liked to think so. I liked to think I had something in common with my husband: both of us had almost been destroyed in our youth by family members. All the more reason that we should stick together and not be too quick to trust others.

In return for his story about the scar, I told Odysseus my own story about almost drowning and being rescued by ducks. He was interested in it, and asked me questions about it, and was sympathetic – everything you would wish a listener to be. 'My poor duckling,' he said, stroking me. 'Don't worry. I would never throw such a precious girl into the ocean.' At which point I did some more weeping, and was comforted in ways that were suitable for a wedding night.

So by the time the morning came, Odysseus and I were indeed friends, as Odysseus had promised we would be. Or let me put it another way: I myself had developed friendly feelings towards him – more than that, loving and passionate ones – and he behaved as if he reciprocated them. Which is not quite the same thing.

After some days had passed, Odysseus announced his intention of taking me and my dowry back with him to Ithaca. My father was annoyed by this – he wanted the old customs kept, he said, which meant that he wanted both of us and our newly gained wealth right there under his thumb. But we had the support of Uncle Tyndareus, whose son-in-law was Helen's husband, the powerful Menelaus, so Icarius had to back down.

You've probably heard that my father ran after our departing chariot, begging me to stay with him, and that Odysseus asked me if I was going to Ithaca with him of my own free will or did I prefer to remain with my father? It's said that in answer I pulled down my veil, being too modest to proclaim in words my desire for my husband, and that a statue was later erected of me in tribute to the virtue of Modesty.

There's some truth to this story. But I pulled down my veil to hide the fact that I was laughing. You have to admit there was something humorous about a father who'd once tossed his own child into the sea capering down the road after that very child and calling, 'Stay with me!'

I didn't feel like staying. At that moment, I could hardly wait to get away from the Spartan court. I hadn't been very happy there, and I longed to begin a new life.

viii

The Chorus Line: If I Was A Princess, A Popular Tune

As Performed by the Maids, with a Fiddle, an Accordion, and a Penny Whistle

First Maid:

If I was a princess, with silver and gold,
And loved by a hero, I'd never grow old:
Oh, if a young hero came a-marrying me,
I'd always be beautiful, happy, and free!

Chorus:

Then sail, my fine lady, on the billowing wave –
The water below is as dark as the grave,
And maybe you'll sink in your little blue boat –
It's hope, and hope only, that keeps us afloat.

Second Maid:
I fetch and I carry, I hear and obey,
It's Yes sir and No ma'am the whole bleeding day;
I smile and I nod with a tear in my eye,
I make the soft beds in which others do lie.

Third Maid:
Oh gods and oh prophets, please alter my life,
And let a young hero take me for his wife!
But no hero comes to me, early or late –
Hard work is my destiny, death is my fate!

Chorus:
Then sail, my fine lady, on the billowing wave –
The water below is as dark as the grave,
And maybe you'll sink in your little blue boat –
It's hope, and hope only, that keeps us afloat.

The Maids all curtsy.

Melantho of the Pretty Cheeks, passing the hat:

Thank you, sir. Thank you. Thank you.
  Thank you. Thank you.

ix

The Trusted Cackle-Hen

The sea voyage to Ithaca was long and frightening, and also nauseating, or at least I found it so. I spent most of the time lying down or throwing up, sometimes both at once. Possibly I had an aversion to the ocean due to my childhood experience, or possibly the sea-god Poseidon was still annoyed by his failure to devour me.

Thus I saw little of the beauties of sky and cloud that Odysseus reported on his rare visits to see how I was feeling. He spent most of the time either at the bow, peering ahead (I imagined) with a hawk-like gaze in order to spot rocks and sea serpents and other dangers, or at the tiller, or directing the ship in some other way – I didn't know how, because I'd never been on a ship before in my life.

I'd gained a great opinion of Odysseus since our wedding day, and admired him immensely, and had an inflated notion of his capabilities – remember, I was fifteen – so I had the highest confidence in him, and considered him to be a sea captain who could not fail.

At last we arrived at Ithaca, and sailed into the harbour, which was surrounded by steep, rocky cliffs. They must have posted lookouts and lit beacons to announce our approach, because the harbour was thronged with people. A certain amount of cheering went on, and a lot of jostling among those who wanted to see what I looked like as I was led ashore – visible proof of the fact that Odysseus had succeeded in his mission, and had brought back a noble bride and the valuable gifts that came with her.

That night there was a feast for the aristocrats of the town. I appeared at it, wearing a shining veil and one of the best embroidered robes I had brought with me, and accompanied by the maid I had also brought. She was a wedding present to me from my father; her name was Actoris, and she was not at all happy to be there in Ithaca with me. She hadn't wanted to leave the luxuries of the Spartan palace and her friends among the servants, and I didn't blame her. As she was not at all young – even my father would not have been so stupid as to send a blooming girl with me, a possible rival for Odysseus's affections, especially since one of her tasks was to stand sentinel every night outside our bedroom door to prevent interruptions – she did not last long. Her death left me all alone in Ithaca, a stranger among strange people.

I did a lot of secluded weeping in those early days. I tried to conceal my unhappiness from Odysseus, as I did not wish to appear unappreciative. And he himself continued to be as attentive and considerate as he had been at first, although his manner was that of an older person to a child. I often caught him studying me, head on one side, chin in hand, as if I were a puzzle; but that was his habit with all, I soon discovered.

He told me once that everyone had a hidden door, which was the way into the heart, and that it was a point of honour with him to be able to find the handles to those doors. For the heart was both key and lock, and he who could master the hearts of men and learn their secrets was well on the way to mastering the Fates and controlling the thread of his own destiny. Not, he hastened to add, that any man could really do that. Not even the gods, he said, were more powerful than the Three Fatal Sisters. He did not mention them by name, but spat to avoid bad luck; and I shivered to think of them in their glum cave, spinning out lives, measuring them, cutting them off.

'Do I have a hidden door into my heart?' I asked in what I hoped was a winsome and flirtatious manner. 'And have you found it?'

At this Odysseus only smiled. 'That is for you to tell me,' he said.

'And do you have a door into your heart as well?' I said. 'And have I found the key?' I blush to recall the simpering tone in which I asked this: it was the kind of wheedling Helen might have done. But Odysseus had turned, and was looking out of the window. 'A ship has entered the harbour,' he said. 'It's not one I know.' He was frowning.

'Are you expecting news?' I asked.

'I'm always expecting news,' he said.

Ithaca was no paradise. It was often windy, and frequently rainy and cold. The nobles were a shabby lot compared with those I was used to, and the palace, although sufficient, was not what you would consider large.

There were indeed a lot of rocks and goats, as I'd been told back home. But there were cows as well, and sheep, and pigs, and grain to make bread, and sometimes a pear or an apple or a fig in season, so we were well supplied at table, and in time I got more used to the place. Also, to have a husband like Odysseus was no mean thing. Everyone in the region looked up to him, and petitioners and those seeking his advice were numerous. Some even came in ships from far away to consult him, as he had a reputation as a man who could undo any complicated knot, though sometimes by tying a more complicated one.

His father, Laertes, and his mother, Anticleia, were still in the palace at that time; his mother had not yet died, worn out by watching and waiting for Odysseus to return and, I suspect, by her own bilious digestive system, and his father had not yet quitted the palace in despair at his son's absence to live in a hovel and penalise himself by farming. All of that would happen once Odysseus had been gone for years, but there was no foreshadowing of it yet.

My mother-in-law was circumspect. She was a prune-mouthed woman, and though she gave me a formal welcome I could tell she didn't approve of me. She kept saying that I was certainly very young. Odysseus remarked dryly that this was a fault that would correct itself in time.

The woman who gave me the most trouble at first was Odysseus's former nurse, Eurycleia. She was widely respected – according to her – because she was so intensely reliable. She'd been in the household ever since Odysseus's father had bought her, and so highly had he valued her that he hadn't even slept with her. 'Imagine that, for a slave-woman!' she clucked to me, delighted with herself. 'And I was very good-looking in those days!' Some of the maids told me that Laertes had refrained, not out of respect for Eurycleia, but from fear of his wife, who would never have given him any peace if he'd taken a concubine. 'That Anticleia would freeze the balls off Helios,' as one of them put it. I knew I should have reprimanded her for impudence, but I couldn't repress my laughter.

Eurycleia made a point of taking me under her wing, leading me about the palace to show me where everything was, and, as she kept saying, 'how we do things here'. I ought to have thanked her for it, with my heart as well as my lips, for there is nothing more embarrassing than to make a slip of manners, thus displaying your ignorance of the customs of those around you. Whether to cover the mouth when you laugh, on what occasions to wear a veil, how much of the face it should conceal, how often to order a bath – Eurycleia was an expert on all such matters. That was lucky, for my mother-in-law, Anticleia – who ought to have taken charge in this way – was content to sit silently and say nothing while I made a fool of myself, a tight little smile on her face. She was happy that her adored son Odysseus had pulled off such a coup – a princess of Sparta was not to be sneezed at – but I think she would have been better pleased if I'd died of seasickness on the way to Ithaca and Odysseus had arrived home with the bridal presents but not the bride. Her most frequent expression to me was, 'You don't look well.'

So I avoided her when I could, and went around with Eurycleia, who was at least friendly. She had a fund of information about all the neighbouring noble families, and in that way I learned a great many discreditable things about them that would be useful to me later on.

She talked all the time, and nobody was the world's expert on Odysseus the way she was. She was full of information about what he liked and how he had to be treated, for hadn't she nursed him at her own breast and tended him when he was an infant and brought him up as a youth? Nobody but she must give him his baths, oil his shoulders, prepare his breakfasts, lock up his valuables, lay out his robes for him, and so on and so forth. She left me with nothing to do, no little office I might perform for my husband, for if I tried to carry out any small wifely task she would be right there to tell me that wasn't how Odysseus liked things done. Even the robes I made for him were not quite right – too light, too heavy, too sturdy, too flimsy. 'It will do well enough for the steward,' she would say, 'but surely not for Odysseus.'

Nonetheless, she tried to be kind to me in her own way. 'We'll have to fatten you up,' she would say, 'so you can have a nice big son for Odysseus! That's your job, you just leave everything else to me.' As she was the nearest thing there was to someone I could talk to – besides Odysseus, that is – I came to accept her in time.

She did make herself invaluable when Telemachus was born. I am honour bound to record that. She said the prayers to Artemis when I was in too much pain to speak, and she held my hands and sponged off my forehead, and caught the baby and washed him, and wrapped him up warmly; for if there was one thing she knew – as she kept telling me – it was babies. She had a special language for them, a nonsense language – 'Uzzy woo,' she would croon to Telemachus when drying him after his bath – 'A google woogle poo!' – and it unsettled me to think of my barrel-chested and deep-voiced Odysseus, so skilled in persuasion, so articulate, so dignified, as an infant lying in her arms and having this gurgling discourse addressed to him.

But I couldn't begrudge her the care she took of Telemachus. Her delight in him was boundless. You'd almost have thought she'd given birth to him herself.

Odysseus was pleased with me. Of course he was. 'Helen hasn't borne a son yet,' he said, which ought to have made me glad. And it did. But on the other hand, why was he still – and possibly always – thinking about Helen?

x

The Chorus Line: The Birth of Telemachus, An Idyll

Nine months he sailed the wine-red seas of
his mother's blood
Out of the cave of dreaded Night, of
sleep,
Of troubling dreams he sailed
In his frail dark boat, the boat of himself,
Through the dangerous ocean of his vast
mother he sailed
From the distant cave where the threads of
men's lives are spun,
Then measured, and then cut short
By the Three Fatal Sisters, intent on their
gruesome handcrafts,
And the lives of women also are twisted
into the strand.

And we, the twelve who were later to die by
his hand
At his father's relentless command,
Sailed as well, in the dark frail boats of
ourselves
Through the turbulent seas of our swollen
and sore-footed mothers
Who were not royal queens, but a motley
and piebald collection,
Bought, traded, captured, kidnapped from
serfs and strangers.

After the nine-month voyage we came to
shore,
Beached at the same time as he was, struck
by the hostile air,
Infants when he was an infant, wailing just
as he wailed,
Helpless as he was helpless, but ten times
more helpless as well,

THE BIRTH OF TELEMACHUS, AN IDYLL

For his birth was longed-for and feasted, as our births were not.
His mother presented a princeling. Our various mothers
Spawned merely, lambed, farrowed, littered,
Foaled, whelped and kittened, brooded, hatched out their clutch.
We were animal young, to be disposed of at will,
Sold, drowned in the well, traded, used, discarded when bloomless.
He was fathered; we simply appeared,
Like the crocus, the rose, the sparrows engendered in mud.

Our lives were twisted in his life; we also were children
When he was a child,
We were his pets and his toythings, mock sisters, his tiny companions.
We grew as he grew, laughed also, ran as he ran,

Though sandier, hungrier, sun-speckled,
most days meatless.
He saw us as rightfully his, for whatever
purpose
He chose, to tend him and feed him, to
wash him, amuse him,
Rock him to sleep in the dangerous boats of
ourselves.

We did not know as we played with him
there in the sand
On the beach of our rocky goat-island, close
by the harbour,
That he was foredoomed to swell to our
cold-eyed teenaged killer.
If we had known that, would we have
drowned him back then?
Young children are ruthless and selfish:
everyone wants to live.

Twelve against one, he wouldn't have stood a chance.
Would we? In only a minute, when nobody else was looking?
Pushed his still-innocent child's head under the water
With our own still-innocent childish nurse-maid hands,
And blamed it on waves. Would we have had it in us?
Ask the Three Sisters, spinning their blood-red mazes,
Tangling the lives of men and women together.
Only they know how events might then have been altered.
Only they know our hearts.
From us you will get no answer.

xi

Helen Ruins My Life

After a time I became more accustomed to my new home, although I had little authority within it, what with Eurycleia and my mother-in-law running all domestic matters and making all household decisions. Odysseus was in control of the kingdom, naturally, with his father, Laertes, sticking his oar in from time to time, either to dispute his son's decisions or to back them up. In other words, there was the standard family push-and-pull over whose word was to carry the most weight. All were agreed on one thing: it was not mine.

Dinnertimes were particularly stressful. There were too many undercurrents, too many sulks and growlings on the part of the men and far too many fraught silences encircling my mother-in-law. When I tried to speak to her she would never look at me while answering, but would address her remarks to a footstool or a table. As befitted conversation with the furniture, these remarks were wooden and stiff.

I soon found it was more peaceful just to keep out of things, and to confine myself to caring for Telemachus, when Eurycleia would let me. 'You're barely more than a child yourself,' she would say, snatching my baby out of my arms. 'Here, I'll tend the little darling for a while. You run along and enjoy yourself.'

But I did not know how to do that. Strolling along the cliffs or by the shore alone like some peasant girl or slave was out of the question: whenever I went out I had to take two of the maids with me – I had a reputation to keep up, and the reputation of a king's wife is under constant scrutiny – but they stayed several paces behind me, as was fitting. I felt like a prize horse on parade, walking in my fancy robes while sailors stared at me and townswomen whispered. I had no friend of my own age and station so these excursions were not very enjoyable, and for that reason they became rarer.

Sometimes I would sit in the courtyard, twisting

wool into thread and listening to the maids laughing and singing and giggling in the outbuildings as they went about their chores. When it was raining I would take up my weaving in the women's quarters. There at least I would have company, as a number of slaves were always at work on the looms. I enjoyed weaving, up to a point. It was slow and rhythmical and soothing, and nobody, even my mother-in-law, could accuse me of sitting idle while I was doing it. Not that she ever said a word to that effect, but there is such a thing as a silent accusation.

I stayed in our room a lot – the room I shared with Odysseus. It was a fine enough room, with a view of the sea, though not so fine as my room back in Sparta. Odysseus had made a special bed in it, one post of which was whittled from an olive tree that had its roots still in the ground. That way, he said, no one would ever be able to move or displace this bed, and it would be a lucky omen for any child conceived there. This bedpost of his was a great secret: no one knew about it except Odysseus himself, and my maid Actoris – but she was dead now – and myself. If the word got around about his post, said Odysseus in a mock-sinister manner, he would know I'd been sleeping with some other man, and then – he said, frowning at me in what was supposed to be a playful way – he would be very cross indeed, and he would have to chop me into little pieces with his sword or hang me from the roof beam.

I pretended to be frightened, and said I would never, never think of betraying his big post.

Actually, I really was frightened.

Nevertheless our best times were spent in that bed. Once he'd finished making love, Odysseus always liked to talk to me. He told me many stories, stories about himself, true, and his hunting exploits, and his looting expeditions, and his special bow that nobody but he could string, and how he'd always been favoured by the goddess Athene because of his inventive mind and his skill at disguises and stratagems, and so on, but other stories as well – how there came to be a curse on the House of Atreus, and how Perseus obtained the Hat of Invisibility from Hades and cut off the loathsome Gorgon's head; and how the renowned Theseus and his pal Peirithous had abducted my cousin Helen when she was less than twelve years old and hidden her away, with the intent of casting lots to see which one of them would marry her when she was old enough. Theseus didn't rape her as he might otherwise have done because she was only a child, or so it was said. She was rescued by her two brothers, but not before they'd waged a successful war against Athens to get her back.

This last was a story I already knew, as I'd heard it from Helen herself. It sounded quite different when she told it. Her story was about how Theseus and Peirithous were both so in awe of her divine beauty that they grew faint whenever they looked at her, and could barely come close enough to clasp her knees and beg forgiveness for their audacity. The part of the story she enjoyed the most was the number of men who'd died in the Athenian war: she took their deaths as a tribute to herself. The sad fact is that people had praised her so often and lavished her with so many gifts and adjectives that it had turned her head. She thought she could do anything she wanted, just like the gods from whom – she was convinced – she was descended.

I've often wondered whether, if Helen hadn't been so puffed up with vanity, we might all have been spared the sufferings and sorrows she brought down on our heads by her selfishness and her deranged lust. Why couldn't she have led a normal life? But no – normal lives were boring, and Helen was ambitious. She wanted to make a name for herself. She longed to stand out from the herd.

When Telemachus was a year old, disaster struck. It was because of Helen, as all the world knows by now.

The first we heard of the impending catastrophe was from the captain of a Spartan ship that had docked in our harbour. The ship was on a voyage around our outlying islands, buying and selling slaves, and as was usual with guests of a certain status we entertained the captain to dinner and put him up overnight. Such visitors were a welcome source of news – who had died, who'd been born, who was recently married, who'd killed someone in a duel, who had sacrificed their own child to some god or other – but this man's news was extraordinary.

Helen, he said, had run away with a prince of Troy. This fellow – Paris was his name – was a younger son of King Priam and was understood to be very good looking. It was love at first sight. For nine days of feasting – laid on by Menelaus because of this prince's high standing – Paris and Helen had made moon-eyes at each other behind the back of Menelaus, who hadn't noticed a thing. That didn't surprise me, because the man was thick as a brick and had the manners of a stump. No doubt he hadn't stroked Helen's vanity enough, so she was ripe for someone who would. Then, when Menelaus had to go away to a funeral, the two lovers had simply loaded up Paris's ship with as much gold and silver as they could carry and slipped away.

Menelaus was now in a red rage, and so was his brother Agamemnon because of the slight to the family honour. They'd sent emissaries to Troy, demanding the return of both Helen and the plunder, but these had come back empty-handed. Meanwhile, Paris and the wicked Helen were laughing at them from behind the lofty walls of Troy. It was quite the business, said our guest, with evident relish: like all of us, he enjoyed it when the high and mighty fell flat on their faces. Everyone was talking about it, he said.

As he was listening to this account, Odysseus went white, though he remained silent. That night, however, he revealed to me the cause of his distress. 'We've all sworn an oath,' he said. 'We swore it on the parts of a cut-up sacred horse, so it's a powerful one. Every man who swore it will now be called on to defend the rights of Menelaus, and sail off to Troy, and wage war to get Helen back.' He said it wouldn't be easy: Troy was a great power, a much harder nut to crack than Athens had been when Helen's brothers had devastated it for the same reason.

I repressed a desire to say that Helen should have been kept in a locked trunk in a dark cellar because she was poison on legs. Instead I said, 'Will you have to go?' I was devastated at the thought of having to stay in Ithaca without Odysseus. What joy would there be for me, alone in the palace? By *alone* you will understand that I mean without friends or allies. There would be no midnight pleasures to counterbalance the bossiness of Eurycleia and the freezing silences of my mother-in-law.

'I swore the oath,' said Odysseus. 'In fact, the oath was my idea. It would be difficult for me to get out of it now.'

Nevertheless he did try. When Agamemnon and Menelaus turned up, as they were bound to do – along with a fateful third man, Palamedes, who was no fool, not like the others – Odysseus was ready for them. He'd spread the story around that he'd gone mad, and to back it up he'd put on a ridiculous peasant's hat and was ploughing with an ox and a donkey and sowing the furrows with salt. I thought I was being very clever when I offered to accompany the three visitors to the field to witness this pitiful sight. 'You'll see,' I said, weeping. 'He no longer recognises me, or even our little son!' I carried the baby along with me to make the point.

It was Palamedes who found Odysseus out – he grabbed Telemachus from my arms and put him down right in front of the team. Odysseus either had to turn aside or run over his own son.

So then he had to go.

The other three flattered him by saying an oracle had decreed that Troy could not fall without his help. That eased his preparations for departure, naturally. Which of us can resist the temptation of being thought indispensable?

xii

Waiting

What can I tell you about the next ten years? Odysseus sailed away to Troy. I stayed in Ithaca. The sun rose, travelled across the sky, set. Only sometimes did I think of it as the flaming chariot of Helios. The moon did the same, changing from phase to phase. Only sometimes did I think of it as the silver boat of Artemis. Spring, summer, fall, and winter followed one another in their appointed rounds. Quite often the wind blew. Telemachus grew from year to year, eating a lot of meat, indulged by all.

We had news of how the war with Troy was going: sometimes well, sometimes badly. Minstrels sang songs about the notable heroes – Achilles, Ajax, Agamemnon, Menelaus, Hector, Aeneas, and the rest. I didn't care about them: I waited only for news of Odysseus. When would he come back and relieve my boredom? He too appeared in the songs, and

I relished those moments. There he was making an inspiring speech, there he was uniting the quarrelling factions, there he was inventing an astonishing falsehood, there he was delivering sage advice, there he was disguising himself as a runaway slave and sneaking into Troy and speaking with Helen herself, who – the song proclaimed – had bathed him and anointed him with her very own hands.

I wasn't so fond of that part.

Finally, there he was, concocting the stratagem of the wooden horse filled with soldiers. And then – the news flashed from beacon to beacon – Troy had fallen. There were reports of a great slaughtering and looting in the city. The streets ran red with blood, the sky above the palace turned to fire; innocent boy children were thrown off a cliff, and the Trojan women were parcelled out as plunder, King Priam's daughters among them. And then, finally, the hoped-for news arrived: the Greek ships had set sail for home.

And then, nothing.

* * *

Day after day I would climb up to the top floor of the palace and look out over the harbour. Day after day there was no sign. Sometimes there were ships, but never the ship I longed to see.

Rumours came, carried by other ships. Odysseus and his men had got drunk at their first port of call and the men had mutinied, said some; no, said others, they'd eaten a magic plant that had caused them to lose their memories, and Odysseus had saved them by having them tied up and carried onto the ships. Odysseus had been in a fight with a giant one-eyed Cyclops, said some; no, it was only a one-eyed tavern keeper, said another, and the fight was over non-payment of the bill. Some of the men had been eaten by cannibals, said some; no, it was just a brawl of the usual kind, said others, with ear-bitings and nosebleeds and stabbings and eviscerations. Odysseus was the guest of a goddess on an enchanted isle, said some; she'd turned his men into pigs – not a hard job in my view – but had turned them back into men because she'd fallen in love with him and was feeding him unheard-of delicacies prepared by her own immortal hands, and the two of them made love deliriously every night; no, said others, it was just an expensive whorehouse, and he was sponging off the Madam.

Needless to say, the minstrels took up these themes and embroidered them considerably. They always sang the noblest versions in my presence – the ones in which Odysseus was clever, brave, and resourceful, and battling supernatural monsters, and beloved of goddesses. The only reason he hadn't come back home was that a god – the sea-god Poseidon, according to some – was against him, because a Cyclops crippled by Odysseus was his son. Or several gods were against him. Or the Fates. Or something. For surely – the minstrels implied, by way of praising me – only a strong divine power could keep my husband from rushing back as quickly as possible into my loving – and lovely – wifely arms.

The more thickly they laid it on, the more costly were the gifts they expected from me. I always complied. Even an obvious fabrication is some comfort when you have few others.

My mother-in-law died, wrinkled up like drying mud and sickened by an excess of waiting, convinced that Odysseus would never return. In her mind this was my fault, not Helen's: if only I hadn't carried the baby to the ploughing ground! Old Eurycleia got even older. So did my father-in-law, Laertes. He lost interest in palace life, and went off to the countryside to rummage around on one of his farms, where he could be spotted shambling here and there in grubby clothing and muttering about pear trees. I suspected he was going soft in the head.

Now I was running the vast estates of Odysseus all by myself. In no way had I been prepared for such a task, during my early life at Sparta. I was a princess, after all, and work was what other people did. My mother, although she'd been a queen, had not set a good example. She didn't care for the kinds of meals favoured in the grand palace, since big chunks of meat were the main feature; she preferred

– at the very most – a small fish or two, with seaweed garnish. She had a manner of eating the fish raw, heads first, an activity I would watch with chilled fascination. Have I forgotten to tell you she had rather small pointed teeth?

She disliked ordering the slaves about and punishing them, though she might suddenly kill one who was annoying her – she failed to understand that they had value as property – and she had no use at all for weaving and spinning. 'Too many knots. A spider's work. Leave it to Arachne,' she'd say. As for the chore of supervising the food supplies and the wine cellar and what she called 'the mortal people's golden toys' that were kept in the vast storehouses of the palace, she merely laughed at the thought. 'Naiads can't count past three,' she would say. 'Fish come in shoals, not lists. One fish, two fish, three fish, another fish, another fish, another fish! That's how we count them!' She'd laugh her rippling laugh. 'We immortals aren't misers – we don't hoard! Such things are pointless.' Then she'd slip off to take a dip in the palace fountain, or she'd vanish for days to tell jokes with the dolphins and play tricks on clams.

So in the palace of Ithaca I had to learn from scratch. At first I was impeded in this by Eurycleia, who wanted to be in charge of everything, but finally she realised that there was too much to be done, even for a busybody like her. As the years passed I found myself making inventories – where there are slaves there's bound to be theft, if you don't keep a sharp eye out – and planning the palace menus and wardrobes. Though slave garments were coarse, they did fall apart after a while and had to be replaced, so I needed to tell the spinners and weavers what to make. The grinders of corn were on the low end of the slave hierarchy, and were kept locked in an outbuilding – usually they were put in there for bad behaviour, and sometimes there were fights among them, so I had to be aware of any animosities and vendettas.

The male slaves were not supposed to sleep with the female ones, not without permission. This could be a tricky issue. They sometimes fell in love and became jealous, just like their betters, which could cause a lot of trouble. If that sort of thing got out of hand I naturally had to sell them. But if a pretty child was born of these couplings, I would often keep it and rear it myself, teaching it to be a refined and pleasant servant. Perhaps I indulged some of these children too much. Eurycleia often said so.

Melantho of the Pretty Cheeks was one of these.

Through my steward I traded for supplies, and soon had a reputation as a smart bargainer. Through my foreman I oversaw the farms and the flocks, and made a point of learning about such things as lambing and calving, and how to keep a sow from eating her farrow. As I gained expertise, I came to enjoy the conversations about such uncouth and dirty matters. It was a source of pride to me when my swineherd would come to me for advice.

My policy was to build up the estates of Odysseus so he'd have even more wealth when he came back than when he'd left – more sheep, more cows, more pigs, more fields of grain, more slaves. I had such a clear picture in my mind – Odysseus returning, and me – with womanly modesty – revealing to him how well I had done at what was usually considered a man's business. On his behalf, of course. Always for him. How his face would shine with pleasure! How pleased he would be with me! 'You're worth a thousand Helens,' he would say. Wouldn't he? And then he'd clasp me tenderly in his arms.

Despite all this busyness and responsibility, I felt more alone than ever. What wise counsellors did I have? Who could I depend on, really, except myself? Many nights I cried myself to sleep or prayed to the gods to bring me either my beloved husband or a speedy death. Eurycleia would draw me soothing baths and bring me comforting evening drinks, though these came with a price. She had the irksome habit of reciting folk sayings designed to stiffen my upper lip and encourage me in my dedication and hard work, such as:

She who weeps when sun's in sky
Will never pile the platter high.

or:

She who wastes her time in moan
Will ne'er eat cow when it is grown.

or:

Mistress lazy, slaves get bold,
Will not do what they are told,
Act the thief or whore or knave:
Spare the rod and spoil the slave!

and more of that ilk. If she'd been younger I would have slapped her.

But her exhortations must have had some effect, because during the daytimes I managed to keep up the appearance of cheerfulness and hope, if not for myself, at least for Telemachus. I'd tell him stories of Odysseus – what a fine warrior he was, how clever, how handsome, and how wonderful everything would be once he got home again.

There was an increasing amount of curiosity about

me, as there was bound to be about the wife – or was it the widow? – of such a famous man; foreign ships came to call with more frequency, bringing new rumours. They brought, also, the occasional feeler: if Odysseus were proved to have died, the gods forfend, might I perhaps be open to other offers? Me and my treasures. I ignored these hints, since news of my husband – dubious news, but news – continued to arrive.

Odysseus had been to the Land of the Dead to consult the spirits, said some. No, he'd merely spent the night in a gloomy old cave full of bats, said others. He'd made his men put wax in their ears, said one, while sailing past the alluring Sirens – half-bird, half-woman – who enticed men to their island and then ate them, though he'd tied himself to the mast so he could listen to their irresistible singing without jumping overboard. No, said another, it was a high-class Sicilian knocking shop – the courtesans there were known for their musical talents and their fancy feathered outfits.

It was hard to know what to believe. Sometimes

I thought people were making things up just to alarm me, and to watch my eyes fill with tears. There is a certain zest to be had in tormenting the vulnerable.

Any rumour was better than none, however, so I listened avidly to all. But after several more years the rumours stopped coming altogether: Odysseus seemed to have vanished from the face of the earth.

xiii

The Chorus Line: The Wily Sea Captain, A Sea Shanty

As Performed by the Twelve Maids, in Sailor Costumes

Oh wily Odysseus he set out from Troy,
With his boat full of loot and his heart full
of joy,
For he was Athene's own shiny-eyed boy,
With his lies and his tricks and his thieving!

His first port of call was the sweet Lotus
shore
Where we sailors did long to forget the foul
war;
But we soon were hauled off on the black
ships once more,
Although we were pining and grieving.

To the dread one-eyed Cyclops then next we
did hie,
He wanted to eat us so we put out his eye;
Our lad said, 'I'm No One,' but then
bragged, ''Twas I,
Odysseus, the prince of deceiving!'

So there's a curse on his head from Poseidon
his foe,
That is dogging his heels as he sails to and
fro,
And a big bag of wind that will boisterously
blow
Odysseus, the saltiest seaman!

*Here's a health to our Captain, so gallant and
free,*
Whether stuck on a rock or asleep 'neath a tree,
Or rolled in the arms of some nymph of the sea,
Which is where we would all like to be, man!

The vile Laestrygonians then we did
meet,
Who dined on our men from their brains to
their feet;
He was sorry he'd asked them for something
to eat,
Odysseus, that epical he-man!

On the island of Circe we were turned into
swine,
Till Odysseus bedded the goddess so
fine,
Then he ate up her cakes and he drank up
her wine,
For a year he became her blithe lodger!

So a health to our Captain where'er he may roam,
Tossed here and tossed there on the wide ocean's
foam,
And he's in no hurry to ever get home –
Odysseus, that crafty old codger!

To the Isle of the Dead then he next took
his way,
Filled a trench up with blood, held the
spirits at bay,
Till he learned what Teiresias, the seer, had
to say,
Odysseus, the artfullest dodger!

The Sirens' sweet singing then next he did
brave,
They attempted to lure him to a feathery
grave,
While tied to the mast he did rant and did
rave,
But Odysseus alone learned their riddle!

The whirlpool Charybdis did not our lad
catch,
Nor snake-headed Scylla, she could not him
snatch,

Then he ran the fell rocks that would grind
you to scratch,
For their clashing he gave not a piddle!

We men did a bad turn against his
command,
When we ate the Sun's cattle, they sure
tasted grand,
In a storm we all perished, but our Captain
reached land,
On the isle of the goddess Calypso.

After seven long years there of kissing and
woo,
He escaped on a raft that was drove to and
fro,
Till fair Nausicaa's maids that the laundry
did do,
Found him bare on the beach – he did drip
so!

Then he told his adventures and laid to
his store
A hundred disasters and sufferings galore,
For no one can tell what the Fates have in
store,
Not Odysseus, that master disguiser!

So a health to our Captain, where'er he may be,
Whether walking the earth or adrift on the sea,
For he's not down in Hades, unlike all of we –
And we leave you not any the wiser!

xiv

The Suitors Stuff Their Faces

I was wandering in the fields the other day, if it was a day, nibbling on some asphodel, when I ran into Antinous. He usually struts about in his finest cloak and his best robe, gold brooches and all, looking belligerent and haughty, and shouldering aside the other spirits; but as soon as he sees me he assumes the guise of his own corpse, with blood spurting all down his front and an arrow through his neck.

He was the first of the Suitors that Odysseus shot. This performance of his with the arrow is meant as a reproach, or so he intends it, but it doesn't cut any ice with me. The man was a pest when he was alive, and a pest he remains.

'Greetings, Antinous,' I said to him. 'I wish you'd take that arrow out of your neck.'

'It is the arrow of my love, Penelope of the divine

form, fairest and most sagacious of all women,' he replied. 'Although it came from the renowned bow of Odysseus, in reality the cruel archer was Cupid himself. I wear it in remembrance of the great passion I bore for you, and carried to my grave.' He goes on in this spurious way quite a lot, having had a good deal of practice at it while he was alive.

'Come now, Antinous,' I said. 'We're dead now. You don't have to blather on in this fatuous manner down here – you have nothing to gain by it. There's no need for your trademark hypocrisy. So be a good fellow for once and eject the arrow. It does nothing to improve your appearance.'

He gazed at me lugubriously, with eyes like a whipped spaniel's. 'Merciless in life, merciless in death,' he sighed. But the arrow vanished and the blood disappeared, and his greenish-white complexion returned to normal.

'Thank you,' I said. 'That's better. Now we can be friends, and as a friend you can tell me – why did you Suitors risk your lives by acting in such an outrageous way towards me, and towards Odysseus, not once but for years and years? It's not that you weren't warned. Prophets foretold your doom, and Zeus himself sent bird portents and significant thunderings.'

Antinous sighed. 'The gods wanted to destroy us,' he said.

'That's everyone's excuse for behaving badly,' I said. 'Tell me the truth. It was hardly my divine beauty. I was thirty-five years old by the end of it, worn out with care and weeping, and as we both know I was getting quite fat around the middle. You Suitors weren't born when Odysseus set out for Troy, or else you were mere babies like my son, Telemachus, or you were children at the very most, so for all practical purposes I was old enough to be your mother. You babbled on about how I made your knees melt and how you longed to have me share your bed and bear your children, yet you knew perfectly well that I was all but past child-bearing age.'

'You could probably have still squeezed out one or two little brats,' Antinous replied nastily. He could barely suppress a smirk.

'That's more like it,' I said. 'I prefer straightforward answers. So, what was your real motive?'

'We wanted the treasure trove, naturally,' he said. 'Not to mention the kingdom.' This time he had the impudence to laugh outright. 'What young man wouldn't want to marry a rich and famous widow? Widows are supposed to be consumed with lust, especially if their husbands have been missing or dead for such a long time, as yours was. You weren't exactly a Helen, but we could have dealt with that. The darkness conceals much! All the better that you were twenty years older than us – you'd die first, perhaps with a little help, and then, furnished with your wealth, we could have had our pick of any young and beautiful princess we wanted. You didn't really think we were maddened by love for you, did you? You may not have been much to look at, but you were always intelligent.'

I'd said I preferred straightforward answers, but of course nobody does, not when the answers are so unflattering. 'Thank you for your frankness,' I said coldly. 'It must be a relief to you to express your real feelings for once. You can put the arrow back now. To tell you the truth, I feel a surge of joy every time I see it sticking through your lying, gluttonous neck.'

The Suitors did not appear on the scene right away. For the first nine or ten years of Odysseus's absence we knew where he was – he was at Troy – and we knew he was still alive. No, they didn't start besieging the palace until hope had dwindled and was flickering out. First five came, then ten, then fifty – the more there were, the more were attracted, each fearing to miss out on the perpetual feasting and the marriage lottery. They were like vultures when they spot a dead cow: one drops, then another, until finally every vulture for miles around is tearing up the carcass.

They simply showed up every day at the palace and proclaimed themselves my guests, imposing upon me as their host. Then, taking advantage of my weakness and lack of manpower, they helped themselves to our livestock, butchering the animals themselves, roasting the flesh with the help of their servants, and ordering the maids about and pinching their bottoms as if they were in their own homes. It was astonishing the amount of food they could cram into themselves – they gorged as if their legs were hollow. Each one ate as if to outdo all the others at eating – their goal was to wear down my resistance with the threat of impoverishment, so mountains of meat and hillocks of bread and rivers of wine vanished down their throats as if the earth had opened and swallowed everything down. They said they would continue in this manner until I chose one of them as my new husband, so they punctuated their drunken parties and merrymaking with moronic speeches about my ravishing beauty and my excellence and wisdom.

I can't pretend that I didn't enjoy a certain amount of this. Everyone does; we all like to hear songs in our praise, even if we don't believe them. But I tried to view their antics as one might view a spectacle or a piece of buffoonery. What new similes might they employ? Which one would pretend, most convincingly, to swoon with rapture at the sight of me? Once in a while I would make an appearance in the hall where they were feasting – backed by two of my maids – just to watch them outdo themselves. Amphinomous usually won on the grounds of good manners, although he was far from being the most vigorous. I have to admit that I occasionally daydreamed about which one I would rather go to bed with, if it came to that.

Afterwards, the maids would tell me what pleasantries the Suitors were exchanging behind my back. They were well positioned to eavesdrop, as they were forced to help serve the meat and drink.

What did the Suitors have to say about me, among themselves? Here are a few samples. *First prize, a week in Penelope's bed, second prize, two weeks in Penelope's bed. Close your eyes and they're all the same – just imagine she's Helen, that'll put bronze in your spear, haha! When's the old bitch going to make up her mind? Let's murder the son, get him out of the way while he's young – the little bastard's starting to get on my nerves. What's to stop one of us from just grabbing the old cow and making off with her? No, lads, that would be cheating. You know our bargain – whoever gets the prize gives out respectable gifts to the others, we're agreed, right? We're all in this together, do or die. You do, she dies, because whoever wins has to fuck her to death, hahaha.*

Sometimes I wondered whether the maids were making some of this up, out of high spirits or just to tease me. They seemed to enjoy the reports they brought, especially when I dissolved in tears and prayed to grey-eyed Athene either to bring Odysseus back or put an end to my sufferings. Then they could dissolve in tears as well, and weep and wail, and bring me comforting drinks. It was a relief to their nerves.

Eurycleia was especially diligent in the reporting of malicious gossip, whether true or invented: most probably she was trying to harden my heart against the Suitors and their ardent pleas, so I would remain faithful to the very last gasp. She was always Odysseus's biggest fan.

⋆ ⋆ ⋆

What could I do to stop these aristocratic young thugs? They were at the age when they were all swagger, so appeals to their generosity, attempts to reason with them, and threats of retribution alike had no effect. Not one would back down for fear the others would jeer at him and call him a coward. Remonstrating with their parents did no good: their families stood to gain by their behaviour. Telemachus was too young to oppose them, and in any case he was only one and they were a hundred and twelve, or a hundred and eight, or a hundred and twenty – it was hard to keep track of the number, they were so many. The men who might have been loyal to Odysseus had sailed off with him to Troy, and any of those remaining who might have taken my side were intimidated by the sheer force of numbers, and were afraid to speak up.

I knew it would do no good to try to expel my unwanted suitors, or to bar the palace doors against them. If I tried that, they'd turn really ugly and go on the rampage and snatch by force what they were attempting to win by persuasion. But I was the daughter of a Naiad; I remembered my mother's advice to me. *Behave like water*, I told myself. *Don't try to oppose them. When they try to grasp you, slip through their fingers. Flow around them.*

For this reason I pretended to view their wooing favourably, in theory. I even went so far as to encourage one, then another, and to send them secret messages. But, I told them, before choosing among them I had to be satisfied in my mind that Odysseus would never return.

XV

The Shroud

Month by month the pressure on me increased. I spent whole days in my room – not the room I used to share with Odysseus, no, I couldn't bear that, but in a room of my own in the women's quarters. I would lie on my bed and weep, and wonder what on earth I should do. I certainly didn't want to marry any of those mannerless young whelps. But my son, Telemachus, was growing up – he was almost the same age as the Suitors, more or less – and he was starting to look at me in an odd way, holding me responsible for the fact that his inheritance was being literally gobbled up.

How much easier for him it would be if I would just pack up and go back to my father, King Icarius, in Sparta. The chances of my doing that of my own free will were zero: I had no intention of being hurled into the sea a second time. Telemachus initially thought my return to the home palace would be a fine outcome from his point of view, but on second thought – after he'd done the math – he realised that a good part of the gold and silver in the palace would go back with me, as it had been my dowry. And if I stayed in Ithaca and married one of the noble puppies, that puppy would become the king, and his stepfather, and would have authority over him. Being ordered around by a lad no older than himself did not appeal.

Really, the best solution for him would have been a graceful death on my part, one for which he was in no way to blame. For if he did as Orestes had done – but with no cause, unlike Orestes – and murdered his mother, he would attract the Erinyes – the dreaded Furies, snake-haired, dog-headed, bat-winged – and they would pursue him with their barking and hissing and their whips and scourges until they had driven him insane. And since he would have killed me in cold blood, and for the basest of motives – the acquisition of wealth – it would be impossible for him to obtain purification at any shrine, and he would be polluted with my blood until he died a horrible death in a state of raving madness.

A mother's life is sacred. Even a badly behaved mother's life is sacred – witness my foul cousin Clytemnestra, adulteress, butcher of her husband, tormenter of her children – and nobody said I was a badly behaved mother. But I did not appreciate the barrage of surly monosyllables and resentful glances I was getting from my own son.

When the Suitors had started their campaign, I'd reminded them that the eventual return of Odysseus had been foretold by an oracle; but as he failed to turn up, year after year, faith in the oracle began to wear thin. Perhaps it had been misinterpreted, the Suitors declared: oracles were notoriously ambiguous. Even I began to doubt, and at last I had to agree – at least in public – that Odysseus was probably dead. Yet his ghost had never appeared to me in a dream, as would have been proper. I could not quite believe that he would fail to send me word of any kind from Hades, should he happen to have reached that shady realm.

I kept trying to think of a way to postpone the day of decision, without reproach to myself. Finally a scheme occurred to me. When telling the story later I used to say that it was Pallas Athene, goddess of weaving, who'd given me this idea, and perhaps this was true, for all I know; but crediting some god for one's inspirations was always a good way to avoid accusations of pride should the scheme succeed, as well as the blame if it did not.

Here is what I did. I set up a large piece of weaving on my loom, and said it was a shroud for my father-in-law, Laertes, since it would be impious of me not to provide a costly winding sheet for him in the event that he should die. Not until this sacred work was finished could I even think of choosing a new husband, but once it was completed I would speedily select the lucky man.

(Laertes was not very pleased by this kind thought of mine: after he heard of it he kept away from the palace more than ever. What if some impatient suitor should hasten his end, forcing me to bury Laertes in the shroud, ready or not, and thus precipitating my own wedding?)

No one could oppose my task, it was so extremely pious. All day I would work away at my loom, weaving diligently, and saying melancholy things like, 'This shroud would be a fitter garment for me than for Laertes, wretched that I am, and doomed by the gods to a life that is a living death.' But at night I would undo what I had accomplished, so the shroud never got any bigger.

To help me in this laborious task I chose twelve of my maidservants – the youngest ones, because these had been with me all their lives. I had bought them or acquired them when they were small children, brought them up as playmates for Telemachus, and trained them carefully in everything they would need to know around the palace. They were pleasant girls, full of energy; they were a little loud and giggly sometimes, as all maids are in youth, but it cheered me up to hear them chattering away, and to listen to their singing. They had lovely voices, all of them, and they had been taught well how to use them.

They were my most trusted eyes and ears in the palace, and it was they who helped me to pick away at my weaving, behind locked doors, at dead of night, and by torchlight, for more than three years. Though we had to do it carefully, and talk in whispers, these nights had a touch of festivity about them, a touch – even – of hilarity. Melantho of the Pretty Cheeks smuggled in treats for us to nibble on – figs in season, bread dipped in honeycomb, heated wine in winter. We told stories as we worked away at our task of destruction; we shared riddles; we made jokes. In the flickering light of the torches our daylight faces were softened and changed, and our daylight manners. We were almost like sisters. In the mornings, our eyes darkened by lack of sleep, we'd exchange smiles of complicity, and here and there a quick squeeze of the hand. Their 'Yes ma'ams' and 'No ma'ams' hovered on the edge of laughter, as if neither they nor I could take their servile behaviour seriously.

Unfortunately one of them betrayed the secret of my interminable weaving. I'm sure it was an accident: the young are careless, and she must have let slip a hint or a word. I still don't know which one: down here among the shadows they all go about in a group, and when I approach them they run away. They shun me as if I had done them a terrible injury. But I never would have hurt them, not of my own accord.

The fact that my secret was betrayed was, strictly speaking, my own fault. I told my twelve young maids – the loveliest, the most beguiling – to hang around the Suitors and spy on them, using whatever enticing arts they could invent. No one knew of my instructions but myself and the maids in question; I chose not to share the secret with Eurycleia – in hindsight, a grave mistake.

This plan came to grief. Several of the girls were unfortunately raped, others were seduced, or were hard pressed and decided that it was better to give in than to resist.

It was not unusual for the guests in a large household or palace to sleep with the maids. To provide a lively night's entertainment was considered part of a good host's hospitality, and such a host would magnanimously offer his guests their pick of the girls – but it was most irregular for the servants to be used in this way without the permission of the master of the house. Such an act amounted to thievery.

However, there was no master of the house. So the Suitors helped themselves to the maids in the same way they helped themselves to the sheep and pigs and goats and cows. They probably thought nothing of it.

I comforted the girls as best I could. They felt quite guilty, and the ones that had been raped needed to be tended and cared for. I put this task into the hands of old Eurycleia, who cursed the bad Suitors, and bathed the girls, and rubbed them with my very own perfumed olive oil for a special treat. She grumbled a bit about doing it. Possibly she resented my affection for the girls. She told me I was spoiling them, and they would get ideas above themselves.

'Never mind,' I said to them. 'You must pretend to be in love with these men. If they think you have taken their side, they'll confide in you and we'll know their plans. It's one way of serving your master, and he'll be very pleased with you when he comes home.' That made them feel better.

I even instructed them to say rude and disrespectful things about me and Telemachus, and about Odysseus as well, in order to further the illusion. They threw themselves into this project with a will: Melantho of the Pretty Cheeks was particularly adept at it, and had lots of fun thinking up snide remarks. There is indeed something delightful about being able to combine obedience and disobedience in the same act.

Not that the whole charade was entirely an illusion. Several of them did fall in love with the men who had used them so badly. I suppose it was inevitable. They thought I couldn't see what was going on, but I knew it perfectly well. I forgave them, however. They were young and inexperienced, and it wasn't every slave-girl in Ithaca who could boast of being the mistress of a young nobleman.

But, love or no love, midnight excursions or none, they continued to report to me any useful information they'd found out.

So I foolishly thought myself quite wise. In retrospect I can see that my actions were ill-considered, and caused harm. But I was running out of time, and becoming desperate, and I had to use every ruse and stratagem at my command.

When they found out about the trick I'd played on them with the shroud, the Suitors broke into my quarters at night and caught me at my work. They were very angry, not least because they'd been fooled by a woman, and they made a terrible scene, and I was put on the defensive. I had to promise to finish the shroud as quickly as possible, after which I would without fail choose one of them as a husband.

The shroud itself became a story almost instantly. 'Penelope's web,' it was called; people used to say that of any task that remained mysteriously unfinished. I did not appreciate the term *web*. If the shroud was a web, then I was the spider. But I had not been attempting to catch men like flies: on the contrary, I'd merely been trying to avoid entanglement myself.

xvi

Bad Dreams

Now began the worst period of my ordeal. I cried so much I thought I would turn into a river or a fountain, as in the old tales. No matter how much I prayed and offered up sacrifices and watched for omens, my husband still didn't return. To add to my misery, Telemachus was now of an age to start ordering me around. I'd run the palace affairs almost single-handedly for twenty years, but now he wanted to assert his authority as the son of Odysseus and take over the reins. He started making scenes in the hall, standing up to the Suitors in a rash way that I was certain was going to get him killed. He was bound to embark on some foolhardy adventure or other, as young men will.

Sure enough, he snuck off in a ship to go chasing around looking for news of his father, without even so much as consulting me. It was a terrible insult, but I couldn't dwell on that part of it, because my favourite maids brought me the news that the Suitors, having learned of my son's daring escapade, were sending a ship of their own to lie in wait for him and ambush him and kill him on his return voyage.

It's true that the herald Medon revealed this plot to me as well, just as the songs relate. But I already knew about it from the maids. I had to appear to be surprised, however, because otherwise Medon – who was neither on one side nor the other – would have known I had my own sources of information.

Well, naturally, I staggered around and fell onto the threshold and cried and wailed, and all of my maids – my twelve favourites, and the rest of them – joined in my lamentations. I reproached them all for not having told me of my son's departure, and for not stopping him, until that interfering old biddy Eurycleia confessed that she alone had aided and abetted him. The only reason the two of them hadn't told me, she said, was that they hadn't wanted me to fret. But all would come out fine in the end, she added, because the gods were just.

I refrained from saying I'd seen scant evidence of that so far.

When things get too dismal, and after I've done as much weeping as possible without turning myself into a pond, I have always – fortunately – been able to go to sleep. And when I sleep, I dream. I had a whole run of dreams that night, dreams that have not been recorded, for I never told them to a living soul. In one, Odysseus was having his head bashed in and his brains eaten by the Cyclops; in another, he was leaping into the water from his ship and swimming towards the Sirens, who were singing with ravishing sweetness, just like my maids, but were already stretching out their birds' claws to tear him apart; in yet another, he was making love with a beautiful goddess, and enjoying it very much. Then the goddess turned into Helen; she was looking at me over the bare shoulder of my husband with a malicious little smirk. This last was such a nightmare that it woke me up, and I prayed that it was a false dream sent from the cave of Morpheus through the gate of ivory, not a true one sent through the gate of horn.

I went back to sleep, and at last managed a comforting dream. This one I did relate; perhaps you have heard of it. My sister Iphthime – who was so much older than I was that I hardly knew her, and who had married and moved far away – came into my room and stood by my bed, and told me she had been sent by Athene herself, because the gods didn't want me to suffer. Her message was that Telemachus would return safely.

But when I questioned her about Odysseus – was he alive or dead? – she refused to answer, and slipped away.

So much for the gods not wanting me to suffer. They all tease. I might as well have been a stray dog, pelted with stones or with its tail set alight for their amusement. Not the fat and bones of animals, but our suffering, is what they love to savour.

xvii

The Chorus Line: Dreamboats, A Ballad

Sleep is the only rest we get;
It's then we are at peace:
We do not have to mop the floor
And wipe away the grease.

We are not chased around the hall
And tumbled in the dirt
By every dimwit nobleman
Who wants a slice of skirt.

And when we sleep we like to dream;
We dream we are at sea,
We sail the waves in golden boats,
So happy, clean and free.

In dreams we all are beautiful
In glossy crimson dresses;
We sleep with every man we love,
We shower them with kisses.

They fill our days with feasting,
We fill their nights with song,
We take them in our golden boats
And drift the whole year long.

And all is mirth and kindness,
There are no tears of pain;
For our decrees are merciful
Throughout our golden reign.

But then the morning wakes us up:
Once more we toil and slave,
And hoist our skirts at their command
For every prick and knave.

xviii

News of Helen

Telemachus avoided the ambush set for him, more by good luck than good planning, and reached home in safety. I welcomed him with tears of joy, and so did all the maids. I am sorry to say that my only son and I then had a big fight.

'You have the brains of a newt!' I raged. 'How dare you take one of the boats and go off like that, without even asking permission? You're barely more than a child! You have no experience at commanding a ship! You could have been killed fifty times over, and then what would your father have to say when he gets home? Of course it would be all my fault for not keeping a better eye on you!' and so on.

It was not the right line to take. Telemachus got up on his high horse. He denied that he was a child any longer, and proclaimed his manhood – he'd come back, hadn't he, which was proof enough that he'd known what he was doing. Then he defied my parental authority by saying he didn't need anyone's permission to take a boat that was more or less part of his own inheritance, but it was no thanks to me that he had any inheritance left, since I hadn't defended it and now it was all being eaten up by the Suitors. He then said that he'd made the decision he'd had to make – he'd gone in search of his father, since no one else seemed prepared to lift a finger in that direction. He claimed his father would have been proud of him for showing some backbone and getting out from under the thumbs of the women, who as usual were being overemotional and showing no reasonableness and judgment.

By 'the women', he meant me. How could he refer to his own mother as 'the women'?

What could I do but burst into tears?

I then made the Is-this-all-the-thanks-I-get, you-have-no-idea-what-I've-been-through-for-your-sake, no-woman-should-have-to-put-up-with-this-sort-of-suffering, I-might-as-well-kill-myself speech. But

I'm afraid he'd heard it before, and showed by his folded arms and rolled-up eyes that he was irritated by it, and was waiting for me to finish.

That done, we settled down. Telemachus had a nice bath drawn for him by the maids. They gave him a good scrubbing, and some fresh clothes, and then they brought in a lovely dinner for him and for some friends he'd invited over – Piraeus and Theoclymenus were their names. Piraeus was an Ithacan, and had been in cahoots with my son on his secret voyage. I resolved to have a word with him later, and to speak to his parents about letting him run so wild. Theoclymenus was a stranger. He seemed nice enough, but I made a mental note to find out what I could about his ancestry, because boys the age of Telemachus can so easily get into the wrong company.

Telemachus wolfed down the food and knocked back the wine, and I reproached myself for not having taught him better table manners. Nobody could say I hadn't tried. But every time I'd remonstrated with him, that old hen Eurycleia had interposed. 'Come now, my child, let the boy enjoy his dinner, there'll be all the time in the world for manners once he's grown up', and much more in that vein.

'As the twig is bent, so will the tree grow,' I would say.

'And that's just it!' she would cackle. 'We don't want to *bend* the little twiggie, do we? Oh, nosie nosie no! We want him to grow straight and tall, and get the juicy goodness out of his nice big hunk of meat, without our crosspatch mummy making him all sad!'

Then the maids would giggle, and heap his plate, and tell him what a fine boy he was.

I'm sorry to say he was quite spoiled.

When the three young men had finished eating, I asked about the trip. Had Telemachus found out anything about Odysseus and his whereabouts, that having been the object of his excursion? And if he had indeed discovered something, could he possibly bring himself to share this discovery with me?

You can see things were still a little frosty on my

part. It's hard to lose an argument to one's teenaged son. Once they're taller than you are, you have only your moral authority: a weak weapon at best.

What Telemachus said next surprised me a good deal. After dropping in on King Nestor, who could tell him nothing, he'd gone off to visit Menelaus. Menelaus himself. Menelaus the rich, Menelaus the thickhead, Menelaus of the loud voice, Menelaus the cuckold. Menelaus, the husband of Helen – cousin Helen, Helen the lovely, Helen the septic bitch, root cause of all my misfortunes.

'And did you see Helen?' I asked in a somewhat constricted voice.

'Oh, yes,' he said. 'She gave us a very good dinner.' He then launched into some rigmarole about the Old Man of the Sea, and how Menelaus had learned from this elderly and dubious-sounding gentleman that Odysseus was trapped on the island of a beautiful goddess, where he was forced to make love with her all night, every night.

By this time I'd heard one beautiful-goddess story too many. 'And how was Helen?' I asked.

'She seemed fine,' said Telemachus. 'Everyone told stories about the war at Troy – they were great stories, a lot of fighting and combat and guts spilling out – my father was in them – but when all the old vets started blubbering, Helen spiked the drinks, and then we laughed a lot.'

'No, but,' I said, 'how did she *look*?'

'As radiant as golden Aphrodite,' he said. 'It was a real thrill to see her. I mean, she's so famous, and part of history and everything. She was absolutely everything she's cracked up to be, and more!' He grinned sheepishly.

'She must be getting a little *older*, by now,' I said as calmly as I could. Helen could not possibly still be as radiant as golden Aphrodite! It would not be within nature!

'Oh, well, yeah,' said my son. And now that bond which is supposed to exist between mothers and fatherless sons finally asserted itself. Telemachus looked into my face and read its expression. 'Actually, she did look quite old,' he said. 'Way older than you. Sort of worn out. All wrinkly,' he added.

'Like an old mushroom. And her teeth are yellow. Actually, some of them have fallen out. It was only after we'd had a lot to drink that she still looked beautiful.'

I knew he was lying, but was touched that he was lying for my sake. Not for nothing was he the great-grandson of Autolycus, friend of Hermes the arch-cheat, and the son of wily Odysseus of the soothing voice, fruitful in false invention, persuader of men and deluder of women. Maybe he had some brains after all. 'Thank you for all you have told me, my son,' I said. 'I'm grateful for it. I will now go and sacrifice a basket of wheat, and pray for your father's safe return.'

And that is what I did.

xix

Yelp of Joy

Who is to say that prayers have any effect? On the other hand, who is to say they don't? I picture the gods, diddling around on Olympus, wallowing in the nectar and ambrosia and the aroma of burning bones and fat, mischievous as a pack of ten-year-olds with a sick cat to play with and a lot of time on their hands. 'Which prayer shall we answer today?' they ask one another. 'Let's cast dice! Hope for this one, despair for that one, and while we're at it, let's destroy the life of that woman over there by having sex with her in the form of a crayfish!' I think they pull a lot of their pranks because they're bored.

Twenty years of my prayers had gone unanswered. But, finally, not this one. No sooner had I performed the familiar ritual and shed the familiar tears than Odysseus himself shambled into the courtyard.

The shambling was part of a disguise, naturally. I would have expected no less of him. Evidently he'd appraised the situation in the palace – the Suitors, their wasting of his estates, their murderous intentions towards Telemachus, their appropriation of the sexual services of his maids, and their intended wife-grab – and wisely concluded that he shouldn't simply march in and announce that he was Odysseus, and order them to vacate the premises. If he'd tried that he'd have been a dead man within minutes.

So he was dressed as a dirty old beggar. He could count on the fact that most of the Suitors had no idea what he looked like, having been too young or not even born when he'd sailed away. His disguise was well enough done – I hoped the wrinkles and baldness were part of the act, and not real – but as soon as I saw that barrel chest and those short legs I had a deep suspicion, which became a certainty when I heard he'd broken the neck of a belligerent fellow panhandler. That was his style: stealthy when necessary, true, but he was never against the direct assault method when he was certain he could win.

I didn't let on I knew. It would have been dangerous for him. Also, if a man takes pride in his disguising skills, it would be a foolish wife who would claim to recognise him: it's always an imprudence to step between a man and the reflection of his own cleverness.

Telemachus was in on the deception: I could see that as well. He was by nature a spinner of falsehoods like his father, but he was not yet very good at it. When he introduced the supposed beggar to me, his shuffling and stammering and sideways looks gave him away.

That introduction didn't happen until later. Odysseus spent his first hours in the palace snooping around and being abused by the Suitors, who jeered and threw things at him. Unfortunately I could not tell my twelve maids who he really was, so they continued their rudeness to Telemachus, and joined the Suitors in their insults. Melantho of the Pretty Cheeks was particularly cutting, I was told. I resolved to interpose myself when the time was right, and to tell Odysseus that the girls had been acting under my direction.

When evening came I arranged to see the supposed beggar in the now-empty hall. He claimed to have news of Odysseus – he spun a plausible yarn, and assured me that Odysseus would be home soon, and I shed tears and said I feared it was not so, as travellers had been telling me the same sort of thing for years. I described my sufferings at length, and my longing for my husband – better he should hear all this while in the guise of a vagabond, as he would be more inclined to believe it.

Then I flattered him by consulting him for advice. I was resolved – I said – to bring out the great bow of Odysseus, the one with which he'd shot an arrow through twelve circular axe-handles – an astounding accomplishment – and challenge the Suitors to duplicate the feat, offering myself as the prize. Surely that would bring an end, one way or another, to the intolerable situation in which I found myself. What did he think of that plan?

He said it was an excellent idea.

The songs claim that the arrival of Odysseus and my decision to set the test of the bow and axes coincided by accident – or by divine plan, which was our way of putting it then. Now you've heard the plain truth. I knew that only Odysseus would be able to perform this archery trick. I knew that the beggar was Odysseus. There was no coincidence. I set the whole thing up on purpose.

Growing confidential with the purported seedy tramp, I then related a dream of mine. It concerned my flock of lovely white geese, geese of which I was very fond. I dreamt that they were happily pecking around the yard when a huge eagle with a crooked beak swooped down and killed them all, whereupon I wept and wept.

Odysseus-the-beggar interpreted this dream for me: the eagle was my husband, the geese were the Suitors, and the one would shortly slay the others. He said nothing about the crooked beak of the eagle, or my love for the geese and my anguish at their deaths.

In the event, Odysseus was wrong about the dream. He was indeed the eagle, but the geese were not the Suitors. The geese were my twelve maids, as I was soon to learn to my unending sorrow.

There's a detail they make much of in the songs. I ordered the maids to wash the feet of Odysseus-the-mendicant, and he refused, saying he could only allow his feet to be washed by one who would not deride him for being gnarled and poor. I then proposed old Eurycleia for the task, a woman whose feet were as lacking in aesthetic value as his own. Grumbling, she set to work, not suspecting the booby trap I'd placed ready for her. Soon she found the long scar familiar to her from the many, many times she'd performed the same service for Odysseus. At this point she let out a yelp of joy and upset the basin of water all over the floor, and Odysseus almost throttled her to keep her from giving him away.

The songs say I didn't notice a thing because Athene had distracted me. If you believe that, you'll believe all sorts of nonsense. In reality I'd turned my back on the two of them to hide my silent laughter at the success of my little surprise.

XX

Slanderous Gossip

At this point I feel I must address the various items of slanderous gossip that have been going the rounds for the past two or three thousand years. These stories are completely untrue. Many have said that there's no smoke without fire, but that is a fatuous argument. We've all heard rumours that later proved to be entirely groundless, and so it is with these rumours about me.

The charges concern my sexual conduct. It is alleged, for instance, that I slept with Amphinomus, the politest of the Suitors. The songs say I found his conversation agreeable, or more agreeable than that of the others, and this is true; but it's a long jump from there into bed. It's also true that I led the Suitors on and made private promises to some of them, but this was a matter of policy. Among other things, I used my supposed encouragement to extract expensive gifts from them – scant return for everything they'd eaten and wasted – and I draw your attention to the fact that Odysseus himself witnessed and approved of my action.

The more outrageous versions have it that I slept with all of the Suitors, one after another – over a hundred of them – and then gave birth to the Great God Pan. Who could believe such a monstrous tale? Some songs aren't worth the breath expended on them.

Various commentators have cited my mother-in-law, Anticleia, who said nothing about the Suitors when Odysseus spoke to her spirit on the Island of the Dead. Her silence is taken as proof: if she'd mentioned the Suitors at all, they say, she would have had to mention my infidelity as well. Maybe she did mean to plant a toxic seed in the mind of Odysseus, but you already know about her attitude towards me. It would have been her final acid touch.

Others have noted the fact that I did not dismiss or punish the twelve impudent maids, or shut them up in an outbuilding to grind corn, so I must have been indulging in the same kind of sluttery myself. But I have explained all that.

A more serious charge is that Odysseus didn't reveal himself to me when he first returned. He distrusted me, it is said, and wanted to make sure I wasn't having orgies in the palace. But the real reason was that he was afraid I would cry tears of joy and thus give him away. Similarly, he had me locked in the women's quarters with the rest of the women when he was slaughtering the Suitors, and he relied on Eurycleia's help, not on mine. But he knew me well – my tender heart, my habit of dissolving in tears and falling down on thresholds. He simply didn't want to expose me to dangers and disagreeable sights. Surely that is the obvious explanation for his behaviour.

If my husband had learned of the slanders during our lifetimes, he certainly would have ripped out a few tongues. But there's no sense in brooding over lost opportunities.

xxi

The Chorus Line: The Perils of Penelope, A Drama

Presented by: The Maids

Prologue: Spoken by Melantho of the Pretty Cheeks:

As we approach the climax, grim and gory,
Let us just say: There is another story.
Or several, as befits the goddess Rumour,
Who's sometimes in a good, or else bad, humour.
Word has it that Penelope the Prissy
Was – when it came to sex – no shrinking sissy!
Some said with Amphinomus she was sleeping.
Masking her lust with gales of moans and weeping;

Others, that each and every brisk contender
By turns did have the fortune to upend her,
By which promiscuous acts the goat-god Pan
Was then conceived, or so the fable ran.
The truth, dear auditors, is seldom certain –
But let us take a peek behind the curtain!

Eurycleia: Played by a Maid:
Dear child! I fear you are undone! Alack!
The Master has returned! That's right – he's
back!

Penelope: Played by a Maid:
I knew him as he walked here from afar
By his short legs –

Eurycleia:
And I by his long scar!

Penelope:
And now, dear Nurse, the fat is in the fire –
He'll chop me up for tending my desire!

While he was pleasuring every nymph and beauty,
Did he think I'd do nothing but my duty?
While every girl and goddess he was praising,
Did he assume I'd dry up like a raisin?

Eurycleia:

While you your famous loom claimed to be threading,
In fact you were at work within the bedding!
And now there's ample matter for – beheading!

Penelope:

Amphinomus – quick! Down the hidden stairs!
And I'll sit here, and feign great woes and cares.
Do up my robe! Bind fast my wanton hairs!
Which of the maids is in on my affairs?

Eurycleia:

Only the twelve, my lady, who assisted,
Know that the Suitors you have not resisted.
They smuggled lovers in and out all night;
They drew the drapes, and then they held
the light.
They're privy to your every lawless thrill –
They must be silenced, or the beans they'll
spill!

Penelope:

Oh then, dear Nurse, it's really up to you
To save me, and Odysseus' honour too!
Because he sucked at your now-ancient bust,
You are the only one of us he'll trust.
Point out those maids as feckless and
disloyal,
Snatched by the Suitors as unlawful spoil,
Polluted, shameless, and not fit to be
The doting slaves of such a Lord as he!

Eurycleia:
We'll stop their mouths by sending them to
Hades –
He'll string them up as grubby wicked
ladies!

Penelope:
And I in fame a model wife shall rest –
All husbands will look on, and think him
blessed!
But haste – the Suitors come to do their
wooing,
And I, for my part, must begin boo-hooing!

The Chorus Line, in tap-dance shoes:
Blame it on the maids!
Those naughty little jades!
Hang them high and don't ask why –
Blame it on the maids!

Blame it on the slaves!
The toys of rogues and knaves!

Let them dangle, let them strangle –
Blame it on the slaves!

Blame it on the sluts!
Those poxy little scuts!
We've got the dirt on every skirt –
Blame it on the sluts!

They all curtsy.

xxii

Helen Takes a Bath

I was wandering through the asphodel, musing on times past, when I saw Helen sauntering my way. She was followed by her customary horde of male spirits, all of them twittering with anticipation. She gave them not even a glance, though she was evidently conscious of their presence. She's always had a pair of invisible antennae that twitch at the merest whiff of a man.

'Hello there, little cousin duck,' she said to me with her usual affable condescension. 'I'm on my way to take my bath. Care to join me?'

'We're spirits now, Helen,' I said with what I hoped was a smile. 'Spirits don't have bodies. They don't get dirty. They have no need of baths.'

'Oh, but my reason for taking a bath was always spiritual,' said Helen, opening her lovely eyes very wide. 'I found it so soothing, in the midst of the turmoil. You wouldn't have any idea of how exhausting it is, having such vast numbers of men quarrelling over you, year after year. Divine beauty is such a burden. At least you've been spared that!'

I ignored the sneer. 'Are you going to take off your spirit robes?' I asked.

'We're all aware of your legendary modesty, Penelope,' she replied. 'I'm sure if you ever were to bathe you'd keep your own robes on, as I suppose you did in life. Unfortunately' – here she smiled – 'modesty was not among the gifts given to me by laughter-loving Aphrodite. I do prefer to bathe without my robes, even in the spirit.'

'That would explain the unusually large crowd of spectators you've attracted,' I said, somewhat tersely.

'But is it unusually large?' she asked, with an innocent lift of her eyebrows. 'There are always such throngs of these men. I never count them. I do feel that because so many of them died for me – well, because of me – surely I owe them something in return.'

'If only a peek at what they missed on earth,' I said.

'Desire does not die with the body,' said Helen. 'Only the ability to satisfy it. But a glimpse or two does perk them up, the poor lambs.'

'It gives them a reason to live,' I said.

'You're being witty,' said Helen. 'Better late than never, I suppose.'

'My wittiness, or your bare-naked tits-and-ass bath treat for the dead?' I said.

'You're such a cynic,' said Helen. 'Just because we're not, you know, any more, there's no need to be so negative. And so – so vulgar! Some of us have a giving nature. Some of us like to contribute what we can to the less fortunate.'

'So you're washing their blood off your hands,' I said. 'Figuratively speaking, of course. Making up for all those mangled corpses. I hadn't realised you were capable of guilt.'

This bothered her. She gave a tiny frown. 'Tell me, little duck – how many men did Odysseus butcher because of you?'

'Quite a lot,' I said. She knew the exact number: she'd long since satisfied herself that the total was puny compared with the pyramids of corpses laid at her door.

'It depends on what you call a lot,' said Helen. 'But that's nice. I'm sure you felt more important because of it. Maybe you even felt prettier.' She smiled with her mouth only. 'Well, I'm off now, little duck. I'm sure I'll see you around. Enjoy the asphodel.' And she wafted away, followed by her excited entourage.

xxiii

Odysseus and Telemachus Snuff the Maids

I slept through the mayhem. How could I have done such a thing? I suspect Eurycleia put something in the comforting drink she gave me, to keep me out of the action and stop me from interfering. Not that I would have been in the action anyway: Odysseus made sure all the women were locked securely into the women's quarter.

Eurycleia described the whole thing to me, and to anyone else who would listen. First, she said, Odysseus – still in the guise of a beggar – watched while Telemachus set up the twelve axes, and then while the Suitors failed to string his famous bow. Then he got hold of the bow himself, and after stringing it and shooting an arrow through the twelve axes – thus winning me as his bride for a second time – he shot Antinous in the throat, threw off his disguise, and made mincemeat of every last one of the Suitors, first with arrows, then with spears and swords. Telemachus and two faithful herdsmen helped him; nevertheless it was a considerable feat. The Suitors had a few spears and swords, supplied to them by Melanthius, a treacherous goatherd, but none of this hardware was of any help to them in the end.

Eurycleia told me how she and the other women had cowered near the locked door, listening to the shouts and the sounds of breaking furniture, and the groans of the dying. She then described the horror that happened next.

Odysseus summoned her, and ordered her to point out the maids who had been, as he called it, 'disloyal'. He forced the girls to haul the dead bodies of the Suitors out into the courtyard – including the bodies of their erstwhile lovers – and to wash the brains and gore off the floor, and to clean whatever chairs and tables remained intact.

Then – Eurycleia continued – he told Telemachus to chop the maids into pieces with his sword. But my son, wanting to assert himself to his father, and to show that he knew better – he was at that age – hanged them all in a row from a ship's hawser.

Right after that, said Eurycleia – who could not disguise her gloating pleasure – Odysseus and Telemachus hacked off the ears and nose and hands and feet and genitals of Melanthius the evil goatherd and threw them to the dogs, paying no attention to the poor man's agonised screams. 'They had to make an example of him,' said Eurycleia, 'to discourage any further defections.'

'But which maids?' I cried, beginning to shed tears. 'Dear gods – which maids did they hang?'

'Mistress, dear child,' said Eurycleia, anticipating my displeasure, 'he wanted to kill them all! I had to choose some – otherwise all would have perished!'

'Which ones?' I said, trying to control my emotions.

'Only twelve,' she faltered. 'The impertinent ones. The ones who'd been rude. The ones who used to thumb their noses at me. Melantho of the Pretty

Cheeks and her cronies – that lot. They were notorious whores.'

'The ones who'd been raped,' I said. 'The youngest. The most beautiful.' My eyes and ears among the Suitors, I did not add. My helpers during the long nights of the shroud. My snow-white geese. My thrushes, my doves.

It was my fault! I hadn't told her of my scheme.

'They let it go to their heads,' said Eurycleia defensively. 'It wouldn't have done for King Odysseus to allow such impertinent girls to continue to serve in the palace. He could never have trusted them. Now come downstairs, dear child. Your husband is waiting to see you.'

What could I do? Lamentation wouldn't bring my lovely girls back to life. I bit my tongue. It's a wonder I had any tongue left, so frequently had I bitten it over the years.

Dead is dead, I told myself. I'll say prayers and perform sacrifices for their souls. But I'll have to do it in secret, or Odysseus will suspect me, as well.

* * *

There could be a more sinister explanation. What if Eurycleia was aware of my agreement with the maids – of their spying on the Suitors for me, of my orders to them to behave rebelliously? What if she singled them out and had them killed out of resentment at being excluded and the desire to retain her inside position with Odysseus?

I haven't been able to confront her about it, down here. She's got hold of a dozen dead babies, and is always busy tending them. Happily for her they will never grow up. Whenever I approach and try to engage her in conversation she says, 'Later, my child. Gracious me, I've got my hands full! Look at the itty pretty – a wuggle wuggle woo!'

So I'll never know.

xxiv

The Chorus Line: An Anthropology Lecture

Presented by: The Maids

What is it that our number, the number of the maids – the number twelve – suggests to the educated mind? There are twelve apostles, there are twelve days of Christmas, yes, but there are twelve months, and what does the word *month* suggest to the educated mind? Yes? You, Sir, in the back? Correct! *Month* comes from *moon*, as everyone knows. Oh, it is no coincidence, no coincidence at all, that there were twelve of us, not eleven and not thirteen, and not the proverbial eight maids a-milking!

For we were not simply maids. We were not mere slaves and drudges. Oh no! Surely we had a higher function than that! Could it be that we were not the twelve maids, but the twelve maidens? The twelve moon-maidens, companions of Artemis, virginal but deadly goddess of the moon? Could it be that we were ritual sacrifices, devoted priestesses doing our part, first by indulging in orgiastic fertility-rite behaviour with the Suitors, then purifying ourselves by washing ourselves in the blood of the slain male victims – such heaps of them, what an honour to the Goddess! – and renewing our virginity, as Artemis renewed hers by bathing in a spring dyed with the blood of Actaeon? We would then have willingly sacrificed ourselves, as was necessary, re-enacting the dark-of-the-moon phase, in order that the whole cycle might begin again and the silvery new-moon-goddess rise once more. Why should Iphigenia be credited with selflessness and devotion, more than we?

This reading of the events in question ties in – excuse the play on words – with the ship's hawser from which we dangled, for the new moon is a boat. And then there's the bow that figures so prominently in the story – the curved old-moon bow of Artemis, used to shoot an arrow through twelve axe-heads – twelve! The arrow passed through the loops of their handles, the round, moon-shaped loops! And the hanging itself – think, dear educated minds, of the significance of the hanging! Above the earth, up in the air, connected to the moon-governed sea by an umbilical boat-linked rope – oh, there are too many clues for you to miss it!

What's that, Sir? You in the back? Yes, correct, the number of lunar months is indeed thirteen, so there ought to have been thirteen of us. Therefore, you say – smugly, we might add – that our theory about ourselves is incorrect, since we were only twelve. But wait – there were in fact thirteen! The thirteenth was our High Priestess, the incarnation of Artemis herself. She was none other than – yes! Queen Penelope!

Thus possibly our rape and subsequent hanging represent the overthrow of a matrilineal moon-cult by an incoming group of usurping patriarchal father-god-worshipping barbarians. The chief of them, notably Odysseus, would then claim kingship by marrying the High Priestess of our cult, namely Penelope.

No, Sir, we deny that this theory is merely unfounded feminist claptrap. We can understand your reluctance to have such things brought out into the open – rapes and murders are not pleasant subjects – but such overthrows most certainly took place all around the Mediterranean Sea, as excavations at prehistoric sites have demonstrated over and over.

Surely those axes, so significantly not used as weapons in the ensuing slaughter, so significantly never explained in any satisfactory way by three thousand years of commentary – surely they must have been the double-bladed ritual labrys axes associated with the Great Mother cult among the Minoans, the axes used to lop off the head of the Year King at the end of his term of thirteen lunar months! For the rebelling Year King to use Her own bow to shoot an arrow through Her own ritual life-and-death axes, in order to demonstrate his power over Her – what a desecration! Just as the patriarchal penis takes it upon itself to unilaterally shoot through the . . . But we're getting carried away here.

In the pre-patriarchal scheme of things, there may well have been a bow-shooting contest, but it would have been properly conducted. He who won it would be declared ritual king for a year, and would then be hanged – remember the Hanged Man motif, which survives now only as a lowly Tarot card. He would also have had his genitals torn off, as befits a male drone married to the Queen Bee. Both acts, the hanging and the genital-tearing-off, would have ensured the fertility of the crops. But usurping strongman Odysseus refused to die at the end of his rightful term. Greedy for prolonged life and power, he found substitutes. Genitals were indeed torn off, but they were not his – they belonged to the goatherd Melanthius. Hanging did indeed take place, but it was we, the twelve moon-maidens, who did the swinging in his place.

We could go on. Would you like to see some vase paintings, some carved Goddess cult objects? No?

Never mind. Point being that you don't have to get too worked up about us, dear educated minds. You don't have to think of us as real girls, real flesh and blood, real pain, real injustice. That might be too upsetting. Just discard the sordid part. Consider us pure symbol. We're no more real than money.

XXV

Heart of Flint

I descended the staircase, considering my choices. I'd pretended not to believe Eurycleia when she told me that it was Odysseus who'd killed the Suitors. Perhaps this man was an imposter, I'd said – how would I know what Odysseus looked like now, after twenty years? I was also wondering how I must seem to him. I'd been very young when he'd sailed away; now I was a matron. How could he fail to be disappointed?

I decided to make him wait: I myself had waited long enough. Also I would need time in order to fully disguise my true feelings about the unfortunate hanging of my twelve young maids.

So when I entered the hall and saw him sitting there, I didn't say a thing. Telemachus wasted no time: almost immediately he was scolding me for not giving a warmer welcome to his father. Flinty-hearted, he called me scornfully. I could see he had a rosy little picture in his mind: the two of them siding against me, grown men together, two roosters in charge of the henhouse. Of course I wanted the best for him – he was my son, I hoped he would succeed, as a political leader or a warrior or whatever he wanted to be – but at that moment I wished there would be another Trojan War so I could send him off to it and get him out of my hair. Boys with their first beards can be a thorough pain in the neck.

The hardness of my heart was a notion I was glad to foster, however, as it would reassure Odysseus to know I hadn't been throwing myself into the arms of every man who'd turned up claiming to be him. So I looked at him blankly, and said it was too much for me to swallow, the idea that this dirty, blood-smeared vagabond was the same as my fine husband who had sailed away, so beautifully dressed, twenty years before.

Odysseus grinned – he was looking forward to the big revelation scene, the part where I would say,

'It was you all along! What a terrific disguise!' and throw my arms around his neck. Then he went off to take a much-needed bath. When he came back in clean clothes, smelling a good deal better than when he'd gone, I couldn't resist teasing him one last time. I ordered Eurycleia to move the bed outside the bedroom of Odysseus, and to make it up for the stranger.

You'll recall that one post of this bed was carved from a tree still rooted in the ground. Nobody knew about it except Odysseus, myself, and my maid Actoris, from Sparta, who by that time was long dead.

Assuming that someone had cut through his cherished bedpost, Odysseus lost his temper at once. Only then did I relent, and go through the business of recognizing him. I shed a satisfactory number of tears, and embraced him, and claimed that he'd passed the bedpost test, and that I was now convinced.

And so we climbed into the very same bed where we'd spent a great many happy hours when we were first married, before Helen took it into her head to run off with Paris, lighting the fires of war and bringing desolation to my house. I was glad it was dark by then, as in the shadows we both appeared less wizened than we were.

'We're not spring chickens any more,' I said.

'That which we are, we are,' said Odysseus.

After a little time had passed and we were feeling pleased with each other, we took up our old habits of story-telling. Odysseus told me of all his travels and difficulties – the nobler versions, with the monsters and the goddesses, rather than the more sordid ones with the innkeepers and whores. He recounted the many lies he'd invented, the false names he'd given himself – telling the Cyclops his name was No One was the cleverest of such tricks, though he'd spoiled it by boasting – and the fraudulent life histories he'd concocted for himself, the better to conceal his identity and his intentions. In my turn, I related the tale of the Suitors, and my trick with the shroud of Laertes, and my deceitful encouragings of the Suitors, and the skilful ways in which I'd misdirected them and led them on and played them off against one another.

Then he told me how much he'd missed me, and how he'd been filled with longing for me even when enfolded in the white arms of goddesses; and I told him how very many tears I'd shed while waiting twenty years for his return, and how tediously faithful I'd been, and how I would never have even so much as thought of betraying his gigantic bed with its wondrous bedpost by sleeping in it with any other man.

The two of us were – by our own admission – proficient and shameless liars of long standing. It's a wonder either one of us believed a word the other said.

But we did.

Or so we told each other.

No sooner had Odysseus returned than he left again. He said that, much as he hated to tear himself away from me, he'd have to go adventuring again. He'd been told by the spirit of the seer Teiresias that he would have to purify himself by carrying an oar so far inland that the people there would mistake it for a winnowing fan. Only in that way could he rinse the blood of the Suitors from himself, avoid their vengeful ghosts and their vengeful relatives, and pacify the anger of the sea-god Poseidon, who was still furious with him for blinding his son the Cyclops.

It was a likely story. But then, all of his stories were likely.

xxvi

The Chorus Line: The Trial of Odysseus, as Videotaped by the Maids

Attorney for the Defence: Your Honour, permit me to speak to the innocence of my client, Odysseus, a legendary hero of high repute, who stands before you accused of multiple murders. Was he or was he not justified in slaughtering, by means of arrows and spears – we do not dispute the slaughters themselves, or the weapons in question – upwards of a hundred and twenty well-born young men, give or take a dozen, who, I must emphasise, had been eating up his food without his permission, annoying his wife, and plotting to murder his son and usurp his throne? It has been alleged by my respected colleague that Odysseus was not so justified, since murdering these young men was a gross overreaction to the fact of their having played the gourmand a little too freely in his palace.

Also, it is alleged that Odysseus and/or his heirs or assigns had been offered material compensation for the missing comestibles, and ought to have accepted this compensation peacefully. But this compensation was offered by the very same young men who, despite many requests, had done nothing previously to curb their remarkable appetites, or to defend Odysseus, or to protect his family. They had shown no loyalty to him in his absence; on the contrary. So how dependable was their word? Could a reasonable man expect that they would ever pay a single ox of what they had promised?

And let us consider the odds. A hundred and twenty, give or take a dozen, to one, or – stretching a point – to four, because Odysseus did have accomplices, as my colleague has termed them; that is, he had one barely grown relative and two servants untrained in warfare – what was to prevent these young men from pretending to enter into a settlement with Odysseus, then leaping upon him one dark night when his guard was down and doing him to death? It is our contention that, by seizing the only opportunity Fate was likely to afford him, our generally esteemed client Odysseus was merely acting in self-defence. We therefore ask that you dismiss this case.

Judge: I am inclined to agree.

Attorney for the Defence: Thank you, Your Honour.

Judge: What's that commotion in the back? Order! Ladies, stop making a spectacle of yourselves! Adjust your clothing! Take those ropes off your necks! Sit down!

The Maids: You've forgotten about us! What about *our* case? You can't let him off! He hanged us in cold blood! Twelve of us! Twelve young girls! For nothing!

Judge (to Attorney for the Defence): This is a new charge. Strictly speaking, it ought to be dealt with in a separate trial; but as the two matters appear to be intimately connected, I am prepared to hear arguments now. What do you have to say for your client?

Attorney for the Defence: He was acting within his rights, Your Honour. These were his slaves.

Judge: Nonetheless he must have had some reason. Even slaves ought not to be killed at whim. What had these girls done that they deserved hanging?

Attorney for the Defence: They'd had sex without permission.

Judge: Hmm. I see. With whom did they have the sex?

Attorney for the Defence: With my client's enemies, Your Honour. The very ones who had designs on his wife, not to mention his life.

(Chuckles at his witticism.)

Judge: I take it these were the youngest maids.

Attorney for the Defence: Well, naturally. They were the best-looking and the most beddable, certainly. For the most part.

The Maids laugh bitterly.

Judge (leafing through book: The Odyssey*)*: It's written here, in this book – a book we must needs consult, as it is the main authority on the subject – although it has pronounced unethical tendencies and contains far too much sex and violence, in my opinion – it says right here – let me see – in Book 22, that the maids were raped. The Suitors raped them. Nobody stopped them from doing so. Also, the maids are described as having been hauled around by the Suitors for their foul and/or disgusting purposes. Your client knew all that – he is quoted as having said these things himself. Therefore, the maids were overpowered, and they were also completely unprotected. Is that correct?

Attorney for the Defence: I wasn't there, Your Honour. All of this took place some three or four thousand years before my time.

Judge: I can see the problem. Call the witness Penelope.

Penelope: I was asleep, Your Honour. I was often asleep. I can only tell you what they said afterwards.

Judge: What who said?

Penelope: The maids, Your Honour.

Judge: They said they'd been raped?

Penelope: Well, yes, Your Honour. In effect.

Judge: And did you believe them?

Penelope: Yes, Your Honour. That is, I tended to believe them.

Judge: I understand they were frequently impertinent.

Penelope: Yes, Your Honour, but . . .

Judge: But you did not punish them, and they continued to work as your maids?

Penelope: I knew them well, Your Honour. I was fond of them. I'd brought some of them up, you could say. They were like the daughters I never had. (*Starts to weep.*) I felt so sorry for them! But most maids got raped, sooner or later; a deplorable but common feature of palace life. It wasn't the fact of their being raped that told against them, in the mind of Odysseus. It's that they were raped without permission.

Judge (chuckles): Excuse me, Madam, but isn't that what rape is? Without permission?

Attorney for the Defence: Without permission of their master, Your Honour.

Judge: Oh. I see. But their master wasn't present. So, in effect, these maids were forced to sleep with the Suitors because if they'd resisted they would have been raped anyway, and much more unpleasantly?

Attorney for the Defence: I don't see what bearing that has on the case.

Judge: Neither did your client, evidently. (*Chuckles.*) However, your client's times were not our times. Standards of behaviour were different then. It would be unfortunate if this regrettable but minor incident were allowed to stand as a blot on an otherwise exceedingly distinguished career. Also I do not wish to be guilty of an anachronism. Therefore I must dismiss the case.

The Maids: We demand justice! We demand retribution! We invoke the law of blood guilt! We call upon the Angry Ones!

A troop of twelve Erinyes appear. They have hair made of serpents, the heads of dogs, and the wings of bats. They sniff the air.

The Maids: Oh Angry Ones, Oh Furies, you are our last hope! We implore you to inflict punishment and exact vengeance on our behalf! Be our defenders, we who had none in life! Smell out Odysseus wherever he goes! From one place to another, from one life to another, whatever disguise he puts on, whatever shape he may take, hunt him down! Dog his footsteps, on earth or in Hades, wherever he may take refuge, in songs and in plays, in tomes and in theses, in marginal notes and in appendices! Appear to him in our forms, our ruined forms, the forms of our pitiable corpses! Let him never be at rest!

The Erinyes turn towards Odysseus. Their red eyes flash.

Attorney for the Defence: I call on grey-eyed Pallas Athene, immortal daughter of Zeus, to defend property rights and the right of a man to be the master in his own house, and to spirit my client away in a cloud!

Judge: What's going on? Order! Order! This is a twenty-first-century court of justice! You there, get down from the ceiling! Stop that barking and hissing! Madam, cover up your chest and put down your spear! What's this cloud doing in here? Where are the police? Where's the defendant? Where has everyone gone?

xxvii

Home Life in Hades

I was looking in on your world the other night, making use of the eyes of a channeller who'd gone into a trance. Her client wanted to contact her dead boyfriend about whether she should sell their condominium, but they got me instead. When there's an opening, I frequently jump in to fill it. I don't get out as often as I'd like.

Not that I mean to disparage my hosts, as it were; but still, it's amazing how the living keep on pestering the dead. From age to age it hardly changes at all, though the methods vary. I can't say I miss the Sibyls much – them and their golden boughs, hauling along all sorts of upstarts to traipse around down here, wanting knowledge of the future and upsetting the Shades – but at least the Sibyls had some manners. The magicians and conjurors who came later were worse, though they did take the whole thing seriously.

Today's bunch, however, are almost too trivial to merit any attention whatsoever. They want to hear about stock-market prices and world politics and their own health problems and such stupidities; in addition to which they want to converse with a lot of dead nonentities we in this realm cannot be expected to know. Who is this 'Marilyn' everyone is so keen on? Who is this 'Adolf'? It's a waste of energy to spend time with these people, and so exasperating.

But it's only by peering through such limited keyholes that I'm able to keep track of Odysseus, during those times he's not down here in his own familiar form.

I suppose you know the rules. If we wish to, we can get ourselves reborn, and have another try at life; but first we have to drink from the Waters of Forgetfulness, so our past lives will be wiped from our memories. Such is the theory; but, like all theories, it's only a theory. The Waters of

Forgetfulness don't always work the way they're supposed to. Lots of people remember everything. Some say there's more than one kind of water – that the Waters of Memory are also on tap. I wouldn't know, myself.

Helen has had more than a few excursions. That's what she calls them – 'my little excursions'. 'I've been having such fun,' she'll begin. Then she'll detail her latest conquests and fill me in on the changes in fashion. It was through her that I learned about patches, and sunshades, and bustles, and high-heeled shoes, and girdles, and bikinis, and aerobic exercises, and body piercings, and liposuction. Then she'll make a speech about how naughty she's been and how much uproar she's been causing and how many men she's ruined. Empires have fallen because of her, she's fond of saying.

'I understand the interpretation of the whole Trojan War episode has changed,' I tell her, to take some of the wind out of her sails. 'Now they think you were just a myth. It was all about trade routes. That's what the scholars are saying.'

'Oh, Penelope, you can't still be jealous,' she says. 'Surely we can be friends now! Why don't you come along with me to the upper world, next time I go? We could do a trip to Las Vegas. Girls' night out! But I forgot – that's not your style. You'd rather play the faithful little wifey, what with the weaving and so on. Bad me, I could never do it, I'd die of boredom. But you were always such a homebody.'

She's right. I'll never drink the Waters of Forgetfulness. I can't see the point of it. No: I can see the point, but I don't want to take the risk. My past life was fraught with many difficulties, but who's to say the next one wouldn't be worse? Even with my limited access I can see that the world is just as dangerous as it was in my day, except that the misery and suffering are on a much wider scale. As for human nature, it's as tawdry as ever.

None of this stops Odysseus. He'll drop in down here for a while, he'll act pleased to see me, he'll tell me home life with me was the only thing he ever really wanted, no matter what ravishing beauties he's been falling into bed with or what wild adventures he's been having. We'll take a peaceful stroll, snack on some asphodel, tell the old stories; I'll hear his news of Telemachus – he's a Member of Parliament now, I'm so proud! – and then, just when I'm starting to relax, when I'm feeling that I can forgive him for everything he put me through and accept him with all his faults, when I'm starting to believe that this time he really means it, off he goes again, making a beeline for the River Lethe to be born again.

He does mean it. He really does. He wants to be with me. He weeps when he says it. But then some force tears us apart.

It's the maids. He sees them in the distance, heading our way. They make him nervous. They make him restless. They cause him pain. They make him want to be anywhere and anyone else.

He's been a French general, he's been a Mongolian invader, he's been a tycoon in America, he's been a headhunter in Borneo. He's been a film star, an inventor, an advertising man. It's always ended badly, with a suicide or an accident or a death in battle or an assassination, and then he's back here again.

'Why can't you leave him alone?' I yell at the maids. I have to yell because they won't let me get near them. 'Surely it's enough! He did penance, he said the prayers, he got himself purified!'

'It's not enough for *us*,' they call.

'What more do you want from him?' I ask them. By this time I'm crying. 'Just tell me!'

But they only run away.

Run isn't quite accurate. Their legs don't move. Their still-twitching feet don't touch the ground.

xxviii

The Chorus Line: We're Walking Behind You, A Love Song

Yoo hoo! Mr Nobody! Mr Nameless! Mr Master of Illusion! Mr Sleight of Hand, grandson of thieves and liars!

We're here too, the ones without names. The other ones without names. The ones with the shame stuck onto us by others. The ones pointed at, the ones fingered.

The chore girls, the bright-cheeked girls, the juicy gigglers, the cheeky young wigglers, the young bloodscrubbers.

Twelve of us. Twelve moon-shaped bums, twelve yummy mouths, twenty-four feather-pillow tits, and best of all, twenty-four twitching feet.

Remember us? Of course you do! We brought the water for you to wash your hands, we bathed your feet, we rinsed your laundry, we oiled your shoulders, we laughed at your jokes, we ground your corn, we turned down your cosy bed.

You roped us in, you strung us up, you left us dangling like clothes on a line. What hijinks! What kicks! How virtuous you felt, how righteous, how purified, now that you'd got rid of the plump young dirty dirt-girls inside your head!

You should have buried us properly. You should have poured wine over us. You should have prayed for our forgiveness.

Now you can't get rid of us, wherever you go: in your life or your afterlife or any of your other lives.

We can see through all your disguises: the paths of day, the paths of darkness, whichever paths you take – we're right behind you, following you like a trail of smoke, like a long tail, a tail made of girls, heavy as memory, light as air: twelve accusations, toes skimming the ground, hands tied behind our backs, tongues sticking out, eyes bulging, songs choked in our throats.

Why did you murder us? What had we done to you that required our deaths? You never answered that.

It was an act of grudging, it was an act of spite, it was an honour killing.

Yoo hoo, Mr Thoughtfulness, Mr Goodness, Mr Godlike, Mr Judge! Look over your shoulder! Here we are, walking behind you, close, close by, close as a kiss, close as your own skin.

We're the serving girls, we're here to serve you. We're here to serve you right. We'll never leave you, we'll stick to you like your shadow, soft and relentless as glue. Pretty maids, all in a row.

xxix

Envoi

we had no voice
we had no name
we had no choice
we had one face
one face the same

we took the blame
it was not fair
but now we're here
we're all here too
the same as you

and now we follow
you, we find you
now, we call
to you to you
too wit too woo

too wit too woo
too woo

The Maids sprout feathers, and fly away as owls.

Notes

The main source for *The Penelopiad* was Homer's *Odyssey*, in the Penguin Classics edition, translated by E.V. Rieu and revised by D.C.H. Rieu (1991).

Robert Graves's *The Greek Myths* (Penguin) was crucial. The information about Penelope's ancestry, her family relations – Helen of Troy was her cousin – and much else, including the stories about her possible infidelity, are to be found there. (See Sections 160 and 171 in particular.) It is to Graves that I owe the theory of Penelope as a possible female-goddess cult leader, though oddly he does not note the significance of the numbers twelve and thirteen in relation to the unfortunate maids. Graves lists numerous sources for the stories and their variants. These sources include Herodotus, Pausanias, Apollodorus, and Hyginus, among many.

The Homeric Hymns were also helpful – especially in relation to the god Hermes – and Lewis Hyde's *Trickster Makes This World* threw some light on the character of Odysseus.

The Chorus of Maids is a tribute to the use of such choruses in Greek drama. The convention of burlesquing the main action was present in the satyr plays performed before serious dramas.

Acknowledgements

Very many thanks to early readers Graeme Gibson, Jess Gibson, Ramsay and Eleanor Cook, Phyllida Lloyd, Jennifer Osti-Fonseca, Surya Bhattacharya, and John Cullen; to my British agents, Vivienne Schuster and Diana McKay, and to my North American agent, Phoebe Larmore; to Louise Dennys of Knopf Canada, who edited with *esprit*; to Heather Sangster, queen of the semi-colons, and to Arnulf Conradi, who sent thought-rays from a distance; to Sarah Cooper and Michael Bradley, for general support and having lunch; to Coleen Quinn, who keeps me in shape; to Gene Goldberg, fastest mouth on the phone; to Eileen Allen and to Melinda Dabaay; and to Arthur Gelgoot Associates. And to Jamie Byng of Canongate, who leapt out from behind a gorse bush in Scotland and talked me into it.